The Leonowens Verandah

THE LEONOWENS VERANDAH

Harry Stephen Deering

LEAPING DEER BOOKS
San Francisco

The Leonowens Verandah

Published by Leaping Deer Books
https://leapingdeerbooks.com

The Leonowens Verandah is a work of fiction. Names, characters, events, and incidents are the product of the author's imagination or are used fictitiously. Any resemblance to actual persons, living or dead, is entirely coincidental.

Print ISBN 978-1-7360908-4-8
Ebook ISBN 978-1-7360908-5-5

Printed in the United States of America

FICTION/ Literary; Fiction/ Historical
1. Thailand 2. Chiang Mai 3. Bangkok 4. Burma 5. Golden Triangle
6. Hill tribes 7. Gymkhana Club 8. Aung San Suu Kyi
9. King Bhumibol Adulyadej 10. Bui doi 11. Luk kreung
12. Brass neck coils 13. The King and I 14. Anna Leonowens

Cover illustrations and map by Richard Sigberman, Corte Madera, CA
Cover and interior design by Gilman Design, Larkspur, CA
Author photo by Stephanie Mohan, Creative Portraiture, Fairfax, CA

For Sheila

CONTENTS

Map of Thailand

CHAPTER ONE

The Queen's Head

TEDDY DINGLE WALKED INTO the Chiang Mai Gymkhana Club, where Jack Quinn was eating an early
lunch. "They've taken out the Queen," Teddy said.

"What are you talking about?" Quinn asked. Teddy, an
elderly British expat, was prone to overstatement and nonsense, often at the same time.

"Come take a look," Teddy said.

Quinn dabbed at sauce on his lips from his Chicken Parmesan and followed Teddy out the back of the club onto
the Leonowens Verandah. The verandah overlooked the
Foreign Cemetery, which the British had established at the
same time they built the Gymkhana Club, in 1898. Amid
the palm trees and glistening red-and-green-tile roofs of the
neighboring Buddhist temples, it seemed inexplicably trans-
ported from another dimension.

In the cemetery was a statue of a pot-bellied Queen Vic-
toria, holding a world globe in the palm of one hand and
clenching a scepter in the other. The queen's head was, in
fact, no longer there.

"What happened?" Quinn asked.

"Taken off in an explosion last night. It's those Red Shirts
again is my guess."

The Red Shirts, country folks from Thailand's Isaan north
and students and progressives from the cities, had been pro-
testing the military junta in Bangkok that had ousted their

1

guy, Prime Minister Thaksin Shinawatra, and his Thai Rak (Thai Love) Party from power several years earlier.

"Seems to me they're just looking for a square deal," Quinn said. Demonstrations in Chiang Mai, almost six hundred kilometers from Bangkok, were small and peaceful; the only threat to public order was the occasional dumpster fire.

But Teddy was personally affronted by the queen's decapitation. He saw it as an attack on British sovereignty.

"Rabble rousers," he huffed. "These people should be grateful for what they've got. Better standard of living than their Vietnamese brethren, to say nothing of those starving Cambodian monkeys. Mobiles and motorbikes—everyone's got one." Teddy was a little guy, no more than five feet, six inches tall and very thin. He yapped like a Chihuahua.

Like many of the expats at the Gymkhana Club, Teddy was a retiree who took a dim view of Thailand and lived there only because their money went farther than in the U.K. That had worked well for a while. The Thais were welcoming, the cost of living was low, and health care was good. The problem began when the British government froze the pensions of those living outside the country. While it was initially tolerable, the Thai *baht* had gained strength against the pound, and inflation got worse. Many elderly expats relying on the National Insurance were finding themselves in a bind. Teddy had been an accountant in gloomy Leeds, and once thought he had moved to paradise. Now it wasn't anymore.

Quinn was an American and didn't care about the queen. He wanted to finish his lunch. When they went back to his table, Teddy hovered.

"Join me?" Quinn asked.

"What's the special?"

"Chicken Parm." He pointed toward his half-eaten meal. The Gymkhana Club did British fare and generic Italian.

Tuesdays was always Chicken Parmesan.

"How much?"

"Two hundred *baht*."

"Six dollars for a scrawny piece of chicken and cheese spread? Outrageous."

"I'm buying," Quinn said.

"Fair enough," said Teddy.

"Want a beer too?" Quinn asked. He was drinking a Singha, the domestic pilsner.

"Since you're having one," Teddy said.

The club's dining room was just off the bar, where Tuang-tong Boonprasan, a twenty-year-old bartender nicknamed Tee, was polishing glasses for gin-and-tonics.

"Interesting drink, the gin-and-tonic," Teddy had said more than once. "Made popular in Singapore by the rubber planters, you know. The quinine provided some prophylaxis against malaria and dengue fever. Some truth to that, I suppose."

"Tee," Teddy yelled, "bring me a Carlsberg."

Quinn grimaced. "I'll have another too, Tee," he said. "Better make it a *yai*."

"Same for me," Teddy said.

Tee brought two big bottles to the table and poured Quinn's first. He knew Quinn was paying and that Teddy always had something unpleasant to say. Today was no exception.

"So what do you think about all this Red Shirt nonsense, *Kuhn* Tee?" he asked, facetiously using the Thai honorific.

"I don't know, *Khun* Teddy," Tee said evenly. "I don't pay much attention to politics. I'm too busy working. And going to school." Tee was studying political science and comparative government at Chiang Mai University.

That was all the opening Teddy needed. "Well, you should start paying attention, young man. They destroyed the Queen's head! Utter impudence! That saxophone-playing king of yours needs to put a stop to this nonsense. Now."

Teddy was referring to King Bhumibol Adulyadej, Rama IX, on the throne for more than fifty years and loved and revered by the people as a Buddhist demigod. Teddy's snarky reference was to the fact that the king was a world-class jazz musician as well. Teddy considered the king soft on crime, as if that were any of his business. He saw the Red Shirts as an affront to his view of world order.

Tee didn't respond to Teddy's badgering. He was doing his best to maintain a cool heart, *jai yen*, but it was obvious he was seething at the attack on the monarch. When he returned to the bar, he commenced to furiously slamming beer bottles into the cooler and hammering ice cubes that didn't need it.

Teddy's comments and attitude were common at the Gymkhana Club. Some in the expat crowd, not just the Brits but Americans and Australians too, routinely carped about everything in Chiang Mai from the lack of proper biscuits at the Tesco Lotus supermarket and the ornamental trees planted in the middle of foot paths to drivers failing to yield to pedestrians, spotty internet reception, and maids who burned holes in your polyester shirts.

"Knock it off, Teddy," Quinn said. "You're a guest in the country, for Chrissakes."

"They're making loads of money off me."

"No, they're not." Teddy was so cheap, it was rumored he took tip money off tables if he thought the patrons were being too generous.

He held up a copy of yesterday's *Bangkok Post*, left behind from the breakfast seating, judging by the marmalade stains. The front page, datelined October 14, 2013, featured a report about the bad air quality caused by rice farmers burning their fields following harvest. Teddy turned the front page

4

toward Quinn and tapped it with an index finger.

"They're ruining the environment too."

Quinn knew that Teddy was a climate-change denier and global-warming skeptic except to the extent these conditions were caused by India, China, and now, apparently, Thailand. Ignoring him, he looked at his already empty glass and went to the bar to get a refill. Behind him, Teddy held up his glass and wagged it.

As Quinn approached the bar, he could see that Tee was still angry, cool heart or no. He was pounding linen napkins into swans with sufficient force to break their long necks. Interspersed among the muttered Thai expletives was a clearly discernible, perfectly articulated "asshole." Tee's parents ran a "Best Pick" hostel that catered to Western backpackers touring Southeast Asia on semester break and during gap years. He spoke vernacular English like an American and routinely said "no problem" rather than "thanks."

"Could we get a couple more beers, small ones, when you get a chance, Tee?"

"Coming right up, *Khun* Jack," he said, quickly regaining his composure.

"Sorry about Teddy."

"*Mai pen rai,*" Tee said, employing an all-purpose Thai phrase that could mean anything from "no big deal" to "don't worry about it" to "it's all good" to "you're excused, *farang*, for your boorish behavior."

Farang was usually a nonpejorative term for foreigners, unless it was intended to be. Like now.

"*Farangs* like Teddy drive us nuts," Tee said. "They need to understand we're not babus, and we're not wogs, and we're not niggers. The British Empire died a long time ago. The sun has finally set. That's why—" He stopped abruptly.

"Why what?"

"Nothing."

5

Quinn brought the beers back to the table. "Drink up," he told Teddy, "I think we've overstayed our welcome."

Tee confirmed that. He whispered something to the other bartender, threw his navy blue barman's vest with the club's Pegasus logo into a laundry hamper, and hurried out the back door.

"You really pissed him off," Quinn said to Teddy. "He could turn you in for *lèse majesté*, you know."

Insulting the king was a major offense in Thailand. One story that had become part of club lore told of the fate of a member who had chased a hundred-*baht* note down a windy street. Thai currency bore the king's image, and after stomping on the note to keep it from blowing away, he received a sentence of five years in the notorious Bang Kwang Central Remand Prison in Bangkok.

It was true, many of the old-timers insisted. It had happened to old Percy Jones, who unfortunately was long since dead and buried in the Foreign Cemetery and so was not available to confirm the tale's veracity. To Quinn, the story seemed apocryphal if you were being polite and bullshit if you were being honest. Even so, accusations of *lèse majesté* were being used more frequently since the coup, especially against protestors calling for reform of the monarchy.

"I'll take my chances," Teddy said, but his eyes showed concern, and his braggadocio quickly gave way to obsessing about crossing a line with the authorities. "He wouldn't really bring me up on charges, would he?"

"You're safe. Tee's a good man."

"You think everyone's a good man, Quinn. Just another sunshine-and-roses Yank is what you are."

This was part of the normal expat exchanges at the Gymkhana Club as well. The Americans mocked the Brits for being supercilious, the Brits laughed at the Americans for their naiveté and instant familiarity, and both scoffed at the loudmouthed Aussies. A few Dutch had joined the club because they were uncomfortable around the Germans. No one liked the French.

"I have to get back to work," Quinn said. The conversation was getting tiresome.

"What's your hurry? Don't you want to take a closer look at the Queen? See what happened?"

Quinn did, actually. He was intrigued by the incident, which had all the earmarks of a high school prank. And a pretty good one at that, he thought. He looked at his watch.

"Sure," he said.

As they walked past the club's billiards room, Teddy said, "Somerset Maugham played snooker here in 1926," pointing to a mahogany table with carved elephant legs and fading green baize. "It's a Burroughs and Wells, turn of the century, brought out from Home." Home. What the Brits had called England from their far-flung colonial outposts in Asia and Africa during the days of empire.

They'd brought gymkhana clubs with them wherever they went: sporting clubs with polo ponies, cricket pitches, tennis courts, long bars, and libraries. Calcutta, Karachi, Singapore, Mombasa. The polo ponies at Chiang Mai were long gone, and most of the clay courts had been overtaken by weeds, but local teams still played cricket, and the rough nine-hole golf course, always struggling for survival against the encroaching jungle, got heavy use. At the back of the club, a hundred-year-old rain tree soared to over sixty feet, its thick green canopy providing welcome shade for drinks at sunset.

As they crossed the verandah, with its rattan chairs facing the golf course, Quinn said abruptly, "I hate that name."

"What name?"

"Leonowens."

The verandah was named for British teak baron Louis

Leonowens, one of the founders of the club and the son of Anna Leonowens, who had brought him to Bangkok as a child in the 1860s, when King Mongkut (Rama IV) hired her to teach English to his children. King Mongkut was a visionary who spoke several European languages, was an expert astronomer and geographer, and led efforts to modernize his country. As portrayed in Margaret Landon's 1944 novel, *Anna and the King of Siam*, and even more in the Broadway musical based on it, *The King and I*, the king was a comic figure, vain, imperious, and subject to the "puzzlement" of Western ways. The book and subsequent movie adaptations were banned in Thailand as unforgivable affronts to a national hero.

"There's nothing wrong with the name," Teddy said as he and Quinn descended the verandah's steps and crossed the putting green to the Foreign Cemetery. "It's fine. Can't rewrite history, you know."

It was straight-up noon, steamy and hot. A few players were desultorily plonking balls into cups on the putting green as the remaining players began coming in from the links, seeking shelter from the sun.

The Foreign Cemetery was the final resting place for the nineteenth-century British entrepreneurs who took the teak, the American Christians who stole the souls, and assorted diplomats, lawyers, schemers, intriguers, and scalawags who tried to take all the rest. Some were innocents, of course, young mothers dying in childbirth, children taken by dengue fever. "Elizabeth Pennell, Devoted Wife and Loving Mother, 1861-1885," read one fading headstone. "Daniel Oliver, A Good Boy. Taken by a snake. 1898-1906," read another.

As they approached the statue, they could see a thin wisp of smoke rising from the queen's neck. Her crowned head lay on the grass several yards away, apparently launched like a missile by the explosion.

Quinn had never read the plaque on the statue until then: "Erected as a token of deep reverence for the memory of the Queen by her loyal subjects of Northern Siam," dated 1913. Quinn found that odd, since he knew that Thailand had never been colonized by any foreign power. Through clever diplomacy, it was the only country in Southeast Asia that hadn't. A bit cheeky on the part of the Brits, he thought.

Two Royal Thai Police officers, in their tight-fitting khakis and high peaked hats, were keeping an eye on the scene from the main gate. They didn't appear concerned. One was chatting up a group of young women on their way to class at the university. The other was texting on his cell phone.

"They should be frisking people," Teddy said, watching the officers let passersby freely enter the cemetery grounds.

"They don't seemed worried."

"Well, they should be worried. By a damn sight, I'd say. Anybody could walk in here."

"It's a public place." Quinn observed the curious *farangs* checking out the scene and the respectful Thais placing marigold garlands and joss sticks at the base of the statue.

"I'm sending a note to the Ambassador. This hooliganism is getting too close to home for my comfort." Teddy was a complaint-filer, letter-to-the-editor writer, demander of his money back, and general nag. His entreaties rarely brought him satisfaction, and usually no response at all, which only made his tetchy demeanor worse.

A local television station, "Action 5 News," had dispatched a film crew. A smartly dressed young reporter who could have been fresh off the set of a major Los Angeles news outlet was interviewing the curious. When she spotted Teddy and Quinn, she scampered over. Her cameraman, lugging his heavy Sony Pro and a shoulder bag full of gear, struggled to keep up.

The reporter approached Teddy and jammed her microphone in his face. "Sir, can you tell us what happened?"

Teddy hid his face behind a hand and barked, "No comment" before scuttling away.

"You, sir?" she said to Quinn.

"Looks like a prank to me."

Not getting enough for a sound bite, the reporter set off to seek more fulsome witness accounts in the growing crowd.

"Does it for me," Quinn said after viewing the commotion for a few more minutes. "Gotta get back to the office."

"I have an appointment too," Teddy said, but Quinn doubted that.

As they left the cemetery through the main gate, they noticed a group of young men across busy Lamphun Road; one of them looked like Tee. A Toyota police truck, roof lights strobing red and blue, was just pulling up.

A sergeant alighted from the truck and started asking questions. It didn't look to Quinn like an arrest as much as a community-policing kind of chat. No one up against the wall, no rough handling, no spread 'em protocol in effect, yet.

"Tee. That little bugger," yelled Teddy. "I knew it was him all along. Too big for his britches if you ask me."

"Nobody did ask. Wait here."

"You bet I will. I'm not getting involved in this."

Quinn dodged traffic crossing the road and smiled at the police sergeant as he approached. "Everything okay, Tee?" he asked.

"No problem, *Kuhn* Jack. They think I might be involved in that," he said, nodding toward the smoldering queen.

After checking IDs, the police sergeant told the detainees to stay put while he ran their names for warrants. Seeing that things appeared to be under control, Teddy crossed the street and confronted Tee.

"What have you done to the Queen, young man?"

"I don't know what you're talking about," Tee said, dispensing with Teddy's name and the polite *Kuhn.*

"I don't believe you," Teddy said. He spun around and stepped back into the road, almost getting hit by a jitney. "Pedestrian right of way!" he shouted at the speeding red truck as he jumped back on the curb.

"So you're okay?" Quinn asked Tee again.

"No worries, *Khun* Jack."

But there were worries after all. A police SUV rolled up, and Tee and two of the others were handcuffed and put in the back seat.

"They just want to talk to us downtown," Tee said to Quinn through the rolled-down window. "No big deal."

When the police sergeant spotted the news crew in the cemetery still trying to get their lead for the six o'clock news, he walked over and offered them a perp walk. He had the young men get out of the car and placed them in the back seat again, this time with a little more force for dramatic effect but making sure their heads were protected.

Once the news segment was a wrap, Quinn handed Tee his business card through the window. The card's logo was a sunshine-yellow pagoda-style schoolhouse filled with young learners raising their hands. "Jack Quinn," the card read, "Program Director, Golden Triangle Education Fund."

"Let me know if I can help," said Quinn.

CHAPTER TWO

Doi Roy

Q UINN LOOKED AT HIS watch again as he left the cemetery dust-up. The afternoon was slipping away. Rather than going in to the office, he decided to work from home, an apartment down a shady *soi* close to the club. It was in an older building that desperately needed fresh paint and grounds maintenance. Once-impressive red bougainvillea was out of control in front; dark mold stains were visible under the window air-conditioning units. It was just off Ratchadamkha Road, and the other expats who lived there referred to it, with only a little affection, as the Damn Rat. But Jack's one-bedroom was comfortable and he liked it, even if the sparse furniture was getting tatty.

As Quinn climbed the stairs to the second-floor unit, he could hear his telephone ringing. He hurriedly fished the door key out of his pocket, hoping he could catch the call before it rolled over to voicemail. As Teddy had mentioned, everyone in Chiang Mai had a cell phone, and the only person who ever called on the land line was Katherine Kerwin, his boss, the chief executive officer of the Golden Triangle Education Fund.

"I've been trying to get ahold of you for hours, Jack," she said. "I thought you were going to be here this afternoon to go over some numbers."

"Got delayed, Kay, sorry."

The Golden Triangle Education Fund was a mostly Amer-

13

ican NGO funded by expats to provide scholarships and build schools for the hill tribes in Thailand's Golden Triangle. Quinn had signed on three months earlier. He had been a lawyer in Seattle and told the GTEF board he was retiring early to head in a totally new direction. He said he found Thailand's Buddhist culture fascinating and that he could get prodigious donations from his book of well-heeled clients.

For some reason, they bought it, but Quinn's major donations were slow to materialize, and now Kay was regularly asking, "Where's the money?" It came in dribs and drabs from friends who Quinn could put the pinch on once or twice, but the cascade of donations he had promised hadn't happened.

The economy is slow, he told her. "Don't worry, things will turn around soon," he said. "Trust me."

"I trust you about as far as I can throw you."

Which wouldn't be far. Quinn was just under six feet tall and still trim, weighing about 180 pounds. Now in his late fifties, he had been an athlete in school and a runner before his knees gave out. His dark hair was beginning to show some gray. Sometimes women gave him a glance. He hadn't yet turned invisible.

Kay was a few years younger, about five-foot-two and fit from the regular tennis she played at the Gymkhana Club. Her blond hair was cut short for the heat, and she dressed in nicely tailored linen skirts and blouses. Quinn thought the gold tennis anklet she sometimes wore was unnecessary but recognized that was none of his business.

Quinn heard a beep on the telephone line.

"Gotta go, Kay," he said. "I've got another call, probably a big fish for me to reel in. I need to take it. See you bright and early in the morning." He hung up before she could reply.

"Hello, Mr. Quinn?" the voice on the line said.

Quinn could visualize the caller, an older male with a

smoker's deep voice. An American, it sounded like. Judging from the sounds of loud music and three-drink laughter, the call probably was from a bar. And was there a slight slur in the caller's voice, Quinn wondered, a swallowed glottal stop here and there? It was just after two in the afternoon.

"My name's Roy Balmer. I run TOP, for Thailand Opportunity Program."

"Never heard of it," Quinn said. It sounded like another struggling do-gooder group like his own. Chiang Mai was full of them. More of them every year, dedicated to causes like adopting elephants and empowering Thai women who really didn't need the help. One group was intent on banning plastic bottles in villages that didn't have running water.

"We're pretty much a one-man show up in Fang, on the Burmese border," the caller continued. "I'm trying to finish building a new school in an Akha village, Baan Nakha. Their old one's falling down. Construction funds are running low."

The disco music began to fade, and the sound of car horns increased. Roy Balmer had apparently moved outside.

"How can I help?" Quinn asked.

"I heard that the Golden Triangle Education Foundation was funding programs. I thought I'd just touch base to see if you guys could help with the school."

"Tell me about your project, and if it sounds promising, maybe we'll take a look. No guarantees." Quinn needed a moneymaker, something that with good marketing could get the donations flowing.

"Understood. Of course. I think you'll like what you see."

"Okay." Quinn had his doubts.

"I've just loaded up on supplies for the school, and I'm heading back north in the morning. Why don't you come along for the ride?" Balmer was articulating his words more clearly now, adrenalin banging against the ethanol, most likely.

15

A site visit would mean missing the Wednesday Quizzes competition at the Gymkhana Club. Quinn usually joined in, often teaming up with Teddy Dingle, whose font of useless information wasn't useless then. But he wouldn't mind avoiding Teddy after their recent interaction. And Balmer's could be just the project they needed.

"Actually, maybe I can do that. What time did you want to leave?"

"Six. It's a five-hour drive. No, wait," Balmer said, hesitating a bit. "Let's make it seven."

Quinn thought that even a seven a.m. start time might be a bit optimistic, given Balmer's apparent rough condition. "Eight?" he asked.

"Even better. Where should we meet?"

Quinn figured Balmer wouldn't be able to find the Damn Rat down its unmarked *soi*. "Do you know the Gymkhana Club?"

"You bet. Drive by it all the time."

"I'll meet you out front."

"Seven sharp."

"Eight."

"Right."

Quinn rang off and sent Kay an email. "Going up north to scout out a very promising Akha project. Sounds like this may be just what we're looking for!" She did not respond.

THE NEXT MORNING, QUINN walked down the still-sleeping *soi*, his camera in his daypack. He didn't get to the Gymkhana Club at eight sharp, as arranged. He had lingered in the shower until the hot water ran out and then had an extra cup of coffee. He figured Balmer would run late anyway. And he did, but not by much. Quinn was waiting under the club's shaded awning when Balmer bounced into the car park at eight-fifteen.

Balmer was driving a black Mitsubishi 4X4 pickup truck that had "Fang Car Hire" painted on the side. He came to a stop precisely in front of where Quinn stood. With the engine still running, he jumped out of the cab, swung around the front, gave Jack a fist bump, and said, "Sorry I'm late." He flung open the passenger door and tossed Quinn's daypack onto the back seat.

Quinn found Balmer to be pretty much as he had envisioned him. In his mid-sixties, probably. He was heavyset and his face was deeply lined, from too much sun or hard living or maybe a combination thereof. His thick gray hair was a bit too long and looked more pruned than cut. His hands were callused and rough, workingman's hands. His cargo shorts, worn short-sleeved shirt, and Australian Blundstone boots would fit on any construction site.

The bed of the truck was covered with a black tarp held securely in place by bungee cords. "Let me show you what I've got," Balmer said, pulling deeply on his cigarette.

He loosened enough straps to reveal some of the payload: primary-level readers, writing paper, packs of pencils, coloring books, and crayons. Also toothbrushes and bundles of brightly colored flip-flops, action figures, and Hello Kitty trinkets.

Quinn had expected hung-over driving and slow reflexes, but Balmer piloted the vehicle with finesse. He never missed a shift and always signaled his lane changes. He checked his mirrors frequently. Quinn had yet to master Thailand's right-hand drive; Balmer had it down.

The hum of the off-road tires and warmth of the morning sun through the windshield had Quinn asleep by the time they reached the new superhighway. He woke an hour later to see Balmer focused on the traffic ahead, leaning over the steering wheel as if to make the loaded pickup go just a bit faster.

"Welcome back," said Balmer, seeing Quinn's eyes blink open.

"Where are we?"

"Chiang Dao."

Quinn looked out the window at white pagoda-roofed houses nestled among terraced green tea fields. "Looks like China," he said, though he had never been there.

"Good call. Some of Chiang Kai-shek's boys fled here when Mao took over in 1949. These guys fought rearguard actions for years. Some of the old vets still wear their Kuomintang uniforms on National Day."

Quinn was surprised not just by Balmer's driving skills but also by his knowledge of the area. He stole a glance at him that did not go undetected.

"What?" Balmer said.

"Just wondering. How did you ever end up here?"

"I more landed up here, kind of like a shipwreck, I guess."

Quinn had learned that the expat code didn't permit prying, but Balmer seemed glad to talk, given the chance.

"Did my time in Vietnam in sixty-eight, and had some troubles when I got home. Maybe they were always there. Too much drinking and drugs. I'm Irish, you know. Addictive personality. Wouldn't call it PTSD exactly. More that I was just fucked up."

That was all Quinn really needed to know, but Balmer wasn't finished.

"Did some VA rehab, and I was okay for years. Had my own construction company in San Diego. Owned my own home. But I couldn't shake the darkness. And bad dreams. In my fifties, I fell off an emotional cliff and left a hellacious mess behind. Lost it all, house and wife. Think Hurricane-Katrina-level disaster."

"So how did you get here? I would think after Vietnam, you'd seen enough of Asia. Why not just go to Mexico?"

18

"I did. Beach at Sayulita. I surfed for a year."

"What happened?"

"Got bored. And the big waves always freaked me out a little, to tell you the truth. But all the downtime got me to reading a lot. I explored religions and spirituality—Islam, Hinduism, Sufism, Zen, you name it. Scientology seemed like bullshit to me. But I noticed that the Dalai Lama always seemed to be smiling. I picked up his book *The Art of Happiness*, and everything clicked. I decided I was a Buddhist and came to Asia to meditate and get closer to God. Dharamsala didn't call to me. The mountains in Thailand did."

"You're not wearing saffron robes."

"No, but," he opened his shirt to reveal a heavy gold Buddhist amulet, "I'm thinking about converting. Hiking through the mountains here may have put me on a right path. I visited lots of villages and got to know the hill tribes. I saw how they were struggling. I saw the need, I had some skills, and I started helping build a school."

They drove on in silence for a few minutes.

Balmer glanced at Quinn. "How about you?"

"Similar story in some ways. Except no war, no explosions. I had a softer landing maybe, but look, here we are. We ended up in the same place. All roads, I guess. Except it sounds like you were an asshole years ago. I was an asshole just last week."

Now they were driving past lime green rice fields so bright, they made your eyes ache. The contrasting dark green mountains of the Chiang Dao range hung off in the distance in a cloudy haze.

"There," said Balmer, pointing toward the highest peak. "That's where we're going." He pulled a cigarette from his pack, the first since they had started driving, more than three hours earlier. "Mind if I smoke?" he asked, lighting up before he got an answer. He inhaled deeply, coughed once, turned his head, and exhaled out the open window.

It was approaching noon, and the extra cup of coffee Quinn had had that morning was burning a hole in his stomach. He needed sustenance. "How about a lunch stop?" he asked.

"Got you covered."

Twenty minutes later, Balmer pulled off the highway in front of an open-air restaurant in the small town of Tha Ton.

"Best catfish stew in the north. They do it with scallions and white pepper. You've never tasted anything like it."

Which was a safe bet. Quinn had never strayed far from safe menu choices like pad Thai and chicken satay. He told himself he was still acclimating to the spicy Thai food. Still, he was surprised that Balmer knew what white pepper was. The man's range was impressive.

They took a table outside the restaurant overlooking the lazy-moving Kok River. A few backpackers were piling onto bamboo rafts for the slow float down to Luang Prabang, in neighboring Laos.

A young boy approached the table. "Some drinks?" he asked.

Quinn didn't hesitate. "Singha," he said.

"Nam soda," Balmer said, opting for carbonated water.

The fish stew arrived quickly and hot. Balmer wafted the steam toward his nose, savoring the aroma. "Hint of ginger," he said.

After one bite, Quinn used a big spoon to get at the thick chunks of fish and shovel sticky rice into his mouth.

"Slow down, Jack," Balmer said. "Enjoy the moment."

"I want to get to the village while it's still light, so I can get some pictures," Quinn said.

"Plenty of time."

Quinn looked at his watch.

Seeing Quinn's impatience, Balmer said, "I'll get my ice

cream to go."

At meal's end, Balmer finished his paper cup of mango-mint in two quick gulps before climbing into the truck. After fastening his seatbelt and cranking the engine back to life, he reached into a breast pocket and tossed Quinn some Dramamine tabs.

"Rough road ahead," he said, reaching into the back seat for a bottled water.

"Tell me more about the Akha tribe," Quinn asked as they resumed their journey.

"Like a lot of the hill tribes, they migrated to Thailand from China and Burma over the past few hundred years," Balmer told him. "They're slash-and-burn farmers, always on the move when the soil plays out. But lately the government is stopping that and settling them in permanent villages. They're not citizens, have no legal rights, and are mostly ignored, except when Bangkok tells them to stop growing opium and switch to soybeans or ornamental flowers or some such thing. Things are getting better, but not fast enough."

CHAPTER THREE

Baan Nakha

T HEY SAILED DOWN SMOOTH highway for another hour, and then Balmer pulled onto the shoulder. Jumping out of the truck, he locked the front hubs into four-wheel-drive, jumped back in, and turned down an unmarked red-dirt road.

More a track than a road, it was deeply rutted from the monsoon rains, and the current dry season had left a slippery surface of fine sand. Shifting into low, low gear, Balmer navigated the vehicle through gulley washes and over stones that scraped the skid plates. He whistled softly to himself and drove with confidence. And some joy.

"Woo hoo!" he yelled as they crested a steep rise and bounced down the other side in a controlled slide.

Quinn wasn't quite so stoked. On his side of the truck, a sheer-rock cliff face was close enough to touch. On Balmer's, the precipice dropped hundreds of feet.

"You should see this when the weather's bad," Balmer said. "It's damn near impassable."

It looked damn near impassable to Quinn right now. He gripped the grab handle for security, as if that would save him if they went over the side.

"How much of this?" he asked.

"Only a few miles. Maybe five."

They crept and bounced along for what seemed like forever to Quinn but was less than an hour by the clock. Eventually,

Balmer took a sharp right down a narrower track that led to a village visible in the shallow valley below.

When they passed under a wooden arch festooned with carved birds, Balmer said, "The spirit gate keeps the good spirits in the village and the bad ones out. The birds fly up to the gods to deliver messages and back down to warn of danger. The Akha are animists, they see spirits in everything. Rocks, trees—kind of like the Cree Indians in North America. But that's another story. The similarities, I mean."

As they drove down into the village, Quinn could see thatched-roofed, bamboo-walled houses, some low to the ground and others on stilts. The buildings had a look of impermanence, reflecting the nomadic lifestyle Balmer had described. Corn was drying on the ground in the common area; women were threshing wheat; men stooped low in the fields, culling shoots of late-season rice. A boy was chasing down a loose pig.

This was not the bucolic scene of village life promised in the guidebooks Quinn had read. The men wore T-shirts, shorts, and flip-flops; the women, drab sarongs. The traditional colorful home-spun jackets, blouses, and leggings were nowhere to be seen. And he didn't notice any laughing grandpas on the porches, exhaling clouds of smoke from thick ganja cigars. The children were beautiful but not particularly well scrubbed.

To his surprise, several of the older kids were tearing around the village on knobby-tired mountain bikes.

"The farang trail-shredders leave them behind when they're done," Balmer said in disgust. More and more young tourists were leaving the beaches in the south and traveling to the jungled north to find new adventures. "The zip lines won't be far behind," he grumbled.

The kids on the bikes were flying off a smooth, rounded concrete mound that looked like a jump or a ramp. "What's

24

that?" Quinn asked.

"I'll explain later."

As Balmer parked the truck in front of the dilapidated schoolhouse, the students came running out, chanting in unison, "*Khun* Roy!" The two teachers, young Akha women, gave Quinn and Balmer a deep *wai*, the traditional Thai greeting: hands together, fingers pointed skyward, heads bowed. The parents hung back, the men with arms folded.

Jumping out of the truck, Balmer shouted a *Sawadee!* greeting to the kids, walked around to the covered truck bed, and unstrapped the tarp. He peeked inside, looked back at the kids, and said "*Peid*?" No response.

One of the teachers smiled and gently corrected his tone for the word "open." The kids affirmed. Loudly.

"May I have your assistance, please," Balmer said to Quinn, now playing the role of magician's aide as they revealed the payload to more cheers.

The children waited in line patiently while the gifts were distributed; then a less orderly secondary market ensued. Red flip-flops were swapped for blue; action figures were traded. The parents loaded the classroom materials onto a cart and wheeled them to the school. The toothbrushes were stacked on a table for distribution after the excitement died down.

"Let me show you the new school site," Balmer told Quinn as the teachers tried to coax the kids back into class.

He led the way to a framed structure still lacking doors and a roof. Inside the shell, Balmer laid out blueprints on a table constructed of planks and sawhorses. The plans revealed a large single-story structure with two classrooms, a kitchen, and a small dormitory for children from neighboring villages. Out back were toilet and shower rooms.

"The whole village can use these," Balmer said, pointing to the newly plumbed lavatories. "Big improvement."

"Who did the plans?"

25

"Students at Chiang Mai U. I know an architecture teacher there. Class project."

Quinn had seen enough. "This is good work, Roy. Looks promising. What do you need to finish?"

"Doors and windows, obviously. It gets cold as hell up here in the winter. Commercial-grade gas stove. A high-output generator and a new satellite dish. The old one is on the fritz."

Quinn thought Balmer was over-asking as a bargaining ploy. "A satellite dish?"

"For school lessons broadcast from Chiang Mai," Balmer said.

"How much is all this going to cost?"

"Twenty thousand dollars, more or less. I can get some stuff donated and some discounted. The Fang Rotary Club helps."

"That might be doable." The price seemed reasonable to Quinn. "I'm not promising anything, understand. We'll need regular reports on progress and expenditures and a hard deadline for completion."

"I can finish it in two months. Three, tops, depending on the weather."

"Make it two."

"Can do."

They walked around the village as it returned to the normal rhythm of agrarian and domestic routine: tilling, minding livestock, the aroma of food cooking on wood stoves, the rattle of hand-powered looms. A few of the older kids were back on their mountain bikes, shooting off the concrete ramp.

"That was before," Balmer said when he saw Quinn looking at the ramp. "I got a cubic yard of ready-mix concrete donated. I meant to get it covered before the rains came. Didn't happen, unfortunately. It got wet, hardened, and turned into a hellacious mess. The kids borrowed my grinder and smoothed it into a ramp. They call it Doi Roy, Roy's Mountain. That kind of thing won't happen again."

"Why not?"

"I don't drop the ball anymore."

Quinn nodded but wondered if that was true. There was no way to know, so he went to the truck, grabbed his camera, gathered smiling kids and teachers, and posed them in front of their falling-down schoolhouse. Perfect for marketing purposes, he thought, and he began shooting away.

The drive back down to Fang from the village felt to Quinn like a post-ballgame recap. The day had been perfect, Balmer pitched well, and the kids hit it out of the park.

"If I get the truck back by six, I won't have to pay for another day," Balmer said as they pulled into town. Which seemed his way of telling Quinn he was on his own to catch a ride back to Chiang Mai.

"No problem. Drop me off at the bus station."

"You can stay at my place. Get a fresh start in the morning. I live nearby." Balmer took a dogleg down an industrial side street and said, "That's my place right there."

He pointed to a squat concrete-block building stuck between an auto-repair shop and a plumbing-supply store. It looked more like a shop than a residence. His yard was filled with varying lengths of pipe, reclaimed lumber, kegs of nails, and rusted metal roofing. A cement mixer with a missing wheel rusted away just inside the front gate. Two motorcycles—sixties-vintage Honda Superhawks, one being cannibalized for parts for the other—sat in the shade of a willow tree. A big dog was sleeping on the porch.

"Plenty of room," Balmer said, "if you don't mind the floor."

"Thanks, but I've got a big day tomorrow in Chiang Mai. I need to share the news with my boss."

Quinn sensed Balmer was relieved when he didn't take

27

him up on his offer. "Suit yourself," Balmer said as he headed to the bus station.

"I'll be in touch in a couple of days," Quinn said as he got out.

"Much appreciated, Jack. I won't let you down."

Balmer gave him a salute and sped off. Quinn hoped he was headed for the car hire and not the Drunken Camellia, the bar they'd passed on the way into town.

CHAPTER FOUR

Busted

Q UINN KNEW THAT BUS stations in Thailand were vibrant affairs, and Fang's was no exception. International pop and reedy Isaan folk songs competed with the blaring departure information from PA speakers on poles. Families gathered in bunches to wave farewell or welcome sojourners home. Vendors hawked iced drinks, chips, CDs, and glossy movie magazines for a long ride. Teenage couples lightly canoodled on benches, saying their goodbyes.

Quinn paid for a first-class ticket, which would get him a seat at the front, where the coach didn't sway and had more leg room to boot. He couldn't escape the blare of kung fu movies played on the overhead video screens. The bus hostess offered him earplugs along with his hot towel, which helped. He promptly fell asleep.

Just as he was drifting into deep REM, his cell phone woke him with the electronic beeps he found annoying but hadn't bothered to change. It was Kay on the line.

"Where are you, Jack? I've been trying to reach you all day." Quinn had heard that before.

"Like I told you, Kay, I was up in an Akha village outside of Fang. No cell reception there. But hey, this project looks solid. May be just what we need to get us jump started. I've got pictures."

"Glad to hear it. But that's not why I'm calling. We got a message at the office from Tee, that nice young barman from

31

the club. He's in jail and says he needs your help. He thinks you're a lawyer."

"I am. Or I was. Did he leave a number?"

"He's in jail, Jack, he doesn't have a number. The police think he may have been involved in this queen's-head business. It's all over the news."

"I think maybe he was involved."

"Shit." That was an uncharacteristic expletive for Kay. "Well, you need to bail him out or something."

"Where are they keeping him?"

"Central Police Station. The big one off of Poklao Road. You need to be there tomorrow morning at nine. Talk to a... wait a minute...here it is, Police Colonel Prasong Wongsarat. That's what Tee told me. That's all I know."

Kay hung up and Quinn was listening to dead air and kung fu movies again.

When the bus pulled in for a rest stop, Quinn bought a copy of the *Bangkok Post* at the newsstand. Back on the bus, he skimmed the international news, tracked the Dow Jones, Shanghai, Tokyo, and FTSE exchanges, and read the sports section. Thailand had just defeated Malaysia in the regional World Cup test trials.

Worrying about Tee, he couldn't get back to sleep. He was still wide awake when the bus arrived at Chiang Mai's inter-province bus station just past midnight. Quinn walked the mile home, figuring the exercise might help him sleep. Once he got to his apartment, he let two Singhas work their magic. He emailed Kay, attaching photos from the village, before he crashed.

AT EIGHT-THIRTY THE next morning, Quinn walked up to Ratchadamkha Road and hailed a tuk-tuk, the ubiquitous three-wheel motor-scooter taxis that farted and buzzed like bees and scattered pedestrians all over town.

"*Bai nai?*" the driver asked as he skidded to a stop.

"Central *Son Au.*" The driver flashed him a look of concern in the rear-view. Police stations were never good news, even for *farangs*. When they arrived, the driver didn't pull into the station parking lot but stopped across the street and gave Quinn a *wai* for good luck when he paid.

As soon as he entered the lobby, Quinn saw Tee in a solitary chair, removed a bit from the dejected, cuffed-to-benches detainees waiting to be booked. A slender, young-looking officer with two gold pips on his epaulets was talking to him.

"Colonel?" Quinn asked as he approached the pair.

"Prasong Wongsarat." He held out a hand. "You must be the American lawyer."

"Jack Quinn, not practicing now." It was getting tiresome to explain.

"Close enough for what we're doing here! How about we chat a bit?"

He walked them to a nearby interrogation room furnished with only a table and chairs. Two on one side, one on the other. The Colonel took the single.

"Relax," he said when they were seated. "This is going to be easy." The business card he handed Quinn, printed in English on one side and Thai on the other, identified Colonel Prasong Wongsarat as "District Commander, Special Operations."

That didn't bode well to Quinn, despite the Colonel's assurances. "What do you do exactly, Colonel?" he asked.

"Oh, a bit of this and a bit of that," he said lightly. From Prasong's English—Quinn knew that Thais used first names in formal address—it was obvious he had spent time in the States.

"Where did you study?"

"Did a masters in criminal justice at Long Beach State."

"You seem young to be a colonel."

"Sometimes it's better to be lucky than good, I guess!" Opening the manila folder in front of him, he said, "So,, Tuanthon Boonprasan. Looks like you've been causing some trouble."

"*Châi*, sir," Tee affirmed, eyes down.

"How'd you know Tee was involved?" Quinn asked.

"Some witnesses said they saw him and his buddies by the statue just before the head blew off. We're getting pressure from the British consulate about this. Some expat is raising hell all the way to Bangkok."

"Teddy Dingle."

"I can't say. All I can tell you is this is not worth our time. We want to make this go away. Quickly."

"How do we do that?"

"I did some checking. I see you're with the Golden Triangle Education Fund. Just an idea here. Let Tuanthon work with you for a while. Have him do something positive. Judges love that. The record will be expunged if he stays out of trouble for a year."

"You can do that?"

"Sure. I told you, I did some checking. He's doing well at university and sounds like a good kid. He just got carried away. We'll get this before the judge this afternoon. He's a friend of mine. Is there some project Tee can work on with you guys?"

"We've got a school project starting up in an Akha village. It's going to take a few months to finish, and our guy up there could use a hand. Do you have any building skills, Tee?"

"A little. I help with maintenance at my parents' hostel." He seemed eager for any means of escape offered.

"Perfect!" the Colonel exclaimed.

"What about my friends?"

"I'm trying to match them up with something too. If I

can't, they'll be picking up trash on the ring road for a year," the Colonel told him.

"When can I start?"

"Up to the judge."

"Can I call my parents?"

"Absolutely. In the meantime, Mr. Quinn, why don't you take Tee out to breakfast or something?"

"Good idea. We'll go to Sweetie Pie."

"Best pancakes in town," the Colonel said.

Outside the police station, Tee took a deep breath of the Chiang Mai city air, none too pure because of the crop burn-offs but an improvement over the jailhouse. He lifted his face toward the morning sun and closed his eyes. Quinn pulled his cell from a pocket of the tropical-weight blue blazer that he seldom wore but had seemed appropriate for an encounter with the law.

"How's Tee?" Kay asked.

"Fine. He's right here."

"So he's out? Terrific. Come on in to the office then. I want to hear about the Akha deal."

"Just one thing. There's a few conditions."

"To what?"

"Tee's release. A few strings attached."

"There's always strings attached."

"Right."

"What are they?"

"Tee's going to be released into our custody."

"You mean your custody."

"No, GTEF's. I told the Colonel Tee could work with us in Baan Nakha. He has some building skills. What do you think? Is the project a go?"

"I saw the pictures you sent from the village last night. Impressive. It looks good if you can vouch for this guy Balmer."

35

"I think he's okay."

"You don't know him. But we need a project, and Tee needs some help."

"So that's a yes?"

"Yes. But this is on you, Jack. This and a whole lot else."

"Got it. We see the judge this afternoon. We're going over to Sweetie Pie for breakfast now. The kid looks famished."

"Say hi to Noi," Kay said.

Noi Mongpet was Kay's tennis partner and friend and the owner of Sweetie Pie. Her parents had run a restaurant in the northeastern city of Khorat, which had a U.S. airbase during the Vietnam War. Seeing the Air Force guys missed cooking from home, they had mastered chicken and waffles, omelets, and Australian-beef burgers and steaks. The war ended, the Americans drew down the troops, and they moved to Chiang Mai to cater to the growing American and European tourist trade. When they retired and moved back to Khorat, Noi took over, and now the menu included a variety of baked goods. She was thinking of opening a second place.

The restaurant was a short walk from the police station, just outside Old Chiang Mai's moated south wall on trendy Nimanhaemin Road. As soon as they walked in, Noi came from behind the counter to greet them, brushing flour off her apron, and softly touched Tee's arm. She had already heard. Noi was an energetic fortyish woman with bright, smiling eyes and hair cut short like Kay's for their morning tennis matches.

"Hello, Jack," she said, giving Quinn both a *wai* and an arm pat. She showed them to Quinn's regular table by the window.

With its red-and-white-checkered tablecloths and copper pans hanging on the walls, Sweetie Pie looked like a diner and had a noisy bustle that made it feel welcoming and vibrant. A waitress brought Tee and Quinn plates of fried eggs, pancakes, and rashers of sizzling bacon. Tee dug in and ate in silence.

Quinn broke it. "What were you thinking?" he asked.

"The head?"

"What else?"

"It was supposed to be a joke. Who even looks at that statue?"

Quinn sighed. "I get it, but you've got to be careful. Everyone's a little on edge these days because of the demonstrations."

"It was supposed to be a joke."

"I get it. I think it's kind of funny. But not everyone does."

"You're right."

"Don't blow things up."

"Got it."

When Tee phoned his parents from the table, Quinn could hear mostly angry voices on the line, first his father, he assumed, and then his mother. Tee said little. Noi brought them slices of peach pie without anyone asking.

The Colonel called precisely at eleven. "We're on," he told Quinn. "The judge will meet with us at noon. The courthouse by White Elephant Gate. Know it?"

"By Three Kings Monument."

"Right. Get there a few minutes early. The judge is a stickler."

"That doesn't sound promising."

"No, he's a good guy. No worries."

Quinn and Tee walked the several blocks to the courts building, where Colonel Prasong was waiting for them in the lobby.

"The judge wants to meet us in his chambers," he said.

Leading them through clusters of plaintiffs and defendants and lawyers with fat briefcases, he took them down a quiet hallway to a door with a nameplate in Thai and Roman script that identified the office of Judge Verapol Tungsawan.

"He studied law at the University of New South Wales," the Colonel said. "Top marks." He knocked softly on the door.

"*Khea su,*" the judge called. "Enter."

Judge Verapol was sitting behind an imposing desk below a red-silk banner depicting the mythical winged Garuda, the national symbol of both Thailand and the king. He wore a blue button-down Oxford shirt and no tie, his robes hanging close by. Rimless gold-frame glasses made him look like a younger king.

The judge stood as they entered the chambers and said to Quinn, "You must be *Khun* Jack. Colonel Prasong tells me you're a lawyer."

"Yes, Your Honor," Quinn said. "That is, I—yes." Why complicate things?

"Long time, no see, Prasong. Keeping order in the kingdom?"

"I'm trying, Your Honor."

"Well, let's get into this. Please, sit down. I looked at Tee's file. I think we can take care of this in short order. You told me you have a plan?"

"Yes, Your Honor," said the Colonel. "We'd like to get Tee into a diversion program. He has a clean record, is a full-time university student, but he may be headed down a wrong path."

"Yes, the queen's head. I saw it on television. Bad business, young man. Very disrespectful. What do you propose, Colonel?"

"Mr. Quinn here represents the Golden Triangle Education Foundation."

Quinn stood. "We're building a school up in an Akha village, Your Honor. Tee could help us on that."

"For how long?"

"The project should take two months, three months, tops," Quinn said, fudging the way Balmer had.

"That sounds about right. What do you think of the idea, Tuanthon?"

Tee stood up and said, "Thank you, Your Honor. I am very sorry, Your Honor. I promise this kind of thing won't ever happen again." Quinn looked for crossed fingers behind his back but didn't see any.

"Make sure that it doesn't. Mr. Quinn, are you and your organization prepared to take responsibility? Supervision? Regular reports to the court?"

"Yes, Your Honor. We already have a man in the village."

"He's reliable?"

"Absolutely." Quinn crossed his fingers behind his back.

"All settled then. I'm releasing Tuanthon to your custody, Mr. Quinn. Before I do, I'd like to speak to this young man alone."

Quinn and the Colonel went out to wait in the hall. Tee emerged a few minutes later.

"What did the judge say?" Quinn asked.

"He told me to stay in school, get serious, and do things the right way."

"Keep your nose clean."

"Pretty much."

CHAPTER FIVE

Tee in Baan Nakha

QUINN NEEDED TO CALL Balmer to tell him the project was on and that Tee was part of the team. He punched in the number, and Balmer picked up on the first ring.

"Good news, Roy, I talked to Kay. We're good to go."

There was momentary silence on the other end. Long enough for the dog to bark once. "Fantastic," Balmer said.

"There are some conditions, like I said. Weekly reports and pictures, accurate accounting for the expenses. We'll get you a credit card. Pretty strict limits."

"Understood."

"One other thing. More good news."

"What's that?"

"I've got someone to help you."

"I don't need babysitting, Jack. You need to trust me if this is going to work."

"Just the opposite. We've got a kid who's had a little scrape with the law. Nothing serious, but he needs some supervision for a while."

"I could use another set of hands, but I have enough trouble looking out for myself. Can he add value?" Balmer suddenly sounded like a major-project honcho.

Quinn puffed a little. "Excellent carpentry skills. Let me put him on the line. His name is Tee. He's right here."

Quinn could hear Balmer begin to suggest there was no

need when he heard Tee say, "*Sawadee, Kuhn* Roy."

Then began a brief conversation of which Quinn could hear only one side.

"Light switches...paint...PVC pipe" were Tee's responses.

"He sounds all right," Balmer said when Tee handed the phone back to Quinn. "When can he start?"

"As soon as you're ready."

"I'm ready now."

"Give us a couple of days, then he'll be on a bus to Fang."

"Tell him this isn't summer camp."

"He already knows."

"I'll have to withdraw from my classes," Tee said once Quinn finished the call, "and tell the Gymkhana Club I won't be tending bar for a while."

"Let's get started then. We'll swing by the Gymkhana Club. You can cancel your classes online, right?"

"Can do."

They tuk-tukked to the Gymkhana and entered just as Major Clive Purcell, British Royal Army (Ret.) and club president, was exiting his office, just off the entrance foyer. Major Purcell was a jovial, personable, dependable but not particularly talented fellow who had failed to rise to colonel in his thirty-year military career. He was in his seventies, portly but his posture was good. His neatly trimmed moustache was flecked with gray.

At his post from early to late, Wednesday through Sunday, he seemed to have found a niche in Chiang Mai where his abilities fully met the demands of the job, although it was never clear exactly what he did all day. The scuttlebutt was that his long hours were an arrangement with his long-suffering wife, who had followed him to far-flung posts around the world and now happily tended the roses in her garden when she wasn't heading up committees at the club.

"Ah, Mr. Quinn," said the Major, straightening his regimental tie. "And young Mr. Tuanthon. I'm frankly surprised to see you here as well! Sounds like you've been up to a little mischief, young man. We all know about it. Saw it on the evening news!"

Tee started to explain or apologize or both, but the Major tut-tutted before he could say anything.

"No mind, no mind! I know what it's like to be young! Drove my Morgan all around the commons during commencement from Sandhurst. Hah!"

"Tee's going to be working with us for a while, Major," Quinn interjected.

"Oh, yes, that schools-relief enterprise you and Mrs. Kerwin are doing. Of course. Good work, that."

"Will I be able to get my job back when my time's served?" Tee asked him.

"No problem there, Tee. I've spoken to the board of governors. A lot of them find your prank quite amusing. Give the old lady a good punch in the nose, right? Well, not Teddy Dingle, of course. He's got a petition going around for your banishment, but nobody much cares what he thinks. You can come back anytime! Good luck to you! Stay in touch!"

Tee look relieved and *waied* the Major. "Thank you, sir," he said.

"Pleasure! Let's just check if we owe you any back wages."

He led them into his office, where everything was orderly: infantry sword and framed guidons hanging on the walls, a picture of his wife on his desk as if he were posted a thousand miles away. From the bottom drawer, he pulled out a thick ledger with tiny, neat handwritten entries.

"Just as I expected!" he said, handing Tee a stack of *baht* notes from his cashbox. "We owe you for last week!"

Tee fanned the bills. "It's too much," he said.

"A little walking-around money!" The Major got up from his desk and walked them to the door.

43

"Oh, and Quinn, Dingle's looking for you. He said you missed Quizzes again. He said he's thinking of cashiering you from the team."

Wherever the Major had been going, he had apparently changed his mind. When Quinn and Tee left his office, he softly closed the office door behind them.

"I need to explain all this to my parents now," Tee said as they left the club.

"I'll come with you. I'd like to meet them, show them you're in good hands, if I can."

"Appreciated, *Kuhn* Jack. They're taking this hard. I've embarrassed the family. They'll want to meet you."

They tuk-tukked back across the river to the Old City, where the Far North Guesthouse was located in an area favored by backpackers. The front of the building was unadorned except for flags from countries around the world, but the inner courtyard was a carefully tended oasis. Teak tables where young travelers gathered to exchange information were scattered around a brilliant flower garden. Hammocks were slung in quiet corners where the newly arrived could sleep off their jet lag. Free tea and iced water were available from ten-gallon dispensers.

In the lobby, a man in his fifties, a more mature version of Tee, was checking in new arrivals. When he saw Tee, he motioned for a staff person to take over. Then he came from behind the counter and stood in front of his son, still not saying a word. Tee gave his father a *wai* with his hands raised to his forehead, a sign of respect usually reserved for monks. He spoke to him in soft tones and at length. Quinn recognized the word *khathot*, which he knew means "I'm sorry."

When Tee gestured for him to join them, his father *waied* Quinn and introduced himself as Mr. Somchai. His English lacked Tee's vernacular phrases but was fluent. The two men thoroughly discussed the terms of Tee's work-release, with

Quinn promising home visits and unlimited phone-call time.
"Thank you, *Kuhn* Jack; please take care of him," Mr. Somchai said. "He will never do a thing like this again."

A door behind the reception area opened, and a woman Quinn took to be Tee's mother gave him an anguished look and promptly closed the door again.

"When will you be leaving?" Mr. Somchai asked Tee, using English for Quinn's benefit.

"Soon. It's up to *Kuhn* Jack."

"Tomorrow or the next day, if that's okay," Quinn said. "We're ready to start building the school, and we're on a tight schedule."

"Tomorrow," Mr. Somchai said, pronouncing it *tummolo*, Thai style.

Quinn looked at Tee. "There's an afternoon bus. Meet me at the station at noon."

"What should I bring?"

"Just some warm clothes. We'll get you work gear in Fang. And bring something to read. You'll have plenty of time to read up there."

Tee nodded. As did his father, who gently guided Tee toward the office door, speaking in a now-gentle tone that suggested forgiveness.

"LOOK FOR AN OLD American guy," Quinn instructed Tee the next day as he boarded the bus. "He'll be riding a motorcycle," he added. "You can't miss him."

And indeed, as Tee descended the steps of the bus in Fang, shading his eyes from the late-afternoon sun, it did not take long to spot a *farang*, a bear of a man who Tee thought would likely scare young children. Balmer, in turn, saw a city boy in a nicer shirt than any he owned.

"You must be Tee," Balmer said, giving him a fist bump.

"*Khun* Roy?" Tee responded, following up with a *wai*.

"Welcome aboard, young man, we're glad to have you!" Balmer grabbed Tee's gym bag and hefted it. "Heavy," he said as they moved toward Balmer's Superhawk.

"Books."

"Maybe we can swap, I brought a bunch too," Balmer said as he placed Tee's bag in a small motorcycle trailer jammed with tools. He glanced at Tee's light trainers. "You'll need some gear," he said. "*Kuhn* Jack said to buy what you need."

They rode to Fang's one sporting goods store, which carried gear for backpackers headed into the mountains. Tee picked out a sleeping bag and a rain shell at Balmer's urging ("It can be cold as hell up there"), plus two sweatshirts, two pair of thick canvas hiking pants, and Blundstone boots like Balmer wore.

The road to Baan Nakha was easier to negotiate on the light motorcycle than in the 4X4, even with the trailer swinging wildly from side to side on sharp curves. Tee glanced at the sheer cliff face and held onto the pillion strap for dear life.

It was dusk when they arrived at Baan Nakha. A few lanterns glowed from inside the houses, but outside, activity had ceased. They bunked down in the old schoolhouse. Balmer hooked up the old satellite dish to get a spotty internet connection and immediately emailed Quinn.

"Arrived safe and sound. Ordered building materials in Fang that will be arriving soon. Tee seems like a nice kid."

IN THE DAYS THAT followed, they quickly fell into a routine, and every Friday, late in the day but without fail, Balmer emailed brief dispatches outlining their progress.

"Regular deliveries of supplies have commenced," he announced a few weeks in. "Shoddy Chinese pipe causing slight delay," he wrote a week later. He attached photos showing a village work crew erecting a blue metal roof, concrete being poured, bathroom fixtures being installed.

"Tee's settling in nicely," Balmer added in an early note. One of his photos showed Tee smiling and wielding a nail gun like a pistol.

On their regular trips into Fang for supplies, Balmer would scrounge a satellite phone and call. Tee usually spoke with Quinn as well.

"The only bad part is the weather; it's freezing up here," he said on one call. Quinn knew that for Thais, "freezing" meant anything below sixty-five degrees Fahrenheit. But Tee continued, "*Kuhn* Roy says we could see frost soon."

On one call, after Balmer's update, Quinn asked, "Can you put Tee on?"

"He's not here." Balmer could hear him suck air so quickly, he thought he would choke. "No, no, hold on, hold on," Balmer said. "No worries, he hasn't flown the coop. He's over at the teachers' house."

"Doing what?"

"They're teaching him Akha. He's a quick study; knows more words than I do already. Oh, and he brought his tablet along with him. The three of them play video games and listen to T-pop. I think one of the teachers, Peu, has a crush on him."

Which Quinn could understand easily enough. Tee was a good-looking kid.

In the evenings, Tee and Balmer usually read, Balmer by a gas lantern and Tee with the LED headlamp he had purchased at the sporting goods store. Balmer's stack of paperbacks on the floor was mostly thrillers: Clancy, Ludlum, a couple of Nesbøs. But Tee noticed one thick hardcover book, an embossed cross on the cover.

"Is it a Christian book?" he asked.

"Sort of," Balmer said. He picked up his worn copy of *The Asian Journal of Thomas Merton.* "Merton was a Trappist monk," he explained. "But the more he studied, the more he became convinced that all religions are pretty much the same. All seekers are looking for the same truth, he says, and all religions are based on some common notions of morality and charity and love. 'Do unto others.' He calls it syncretism—related beliefs across a diverse spectrum. That makes sense to me; from what I've seen, Buddhism and Christianity have a lot in common. That's what Merton preached. No need for squabbles."

"Sounds about right."

"Yes. Did you know Merton died in Bangkok? He had traveled here to discuss Buddhism with the Dalai Lama. You should read him."

He handed the book to Tee.

"Maybe."

"He pushed for justice, and nonviolence in the civil rights movement in the sixties," Balmer added. "He knew Dr. King."

"Okay. I'll take a look."

Tee was holding his own weighty tome. "What's that you've got?" Balmer asked.

Tee held it up to show him the title.

"*Jurisprudence: The Philosophy and Method of Western Law,*" Balmer read. "What do you think?"

"The Greeks are good. I'm not so crazy about Plato's Republic; the Philosopher King sounds too much like an Asian emperor. Aristotle is better—rule of law, justice for all. I'm up to Hobbes and Locke."

"The Enlightenment."

"Some call it that."

"What do you think?"

"I guess mostly I see a lot of similarities between Eastern and Western thought. Even Lao Tzu talked about a benevolent emperor who respected individual rights. I guess it's all about social harmony and how best to achieve it. Kind of like what you're talking about with Thomas Merton."

"That's it."

"Same same but different," Tee said, using a common Thai phrase noting an unexpected similarity between Thai and Western cultures.

CHAPTER SIX

The Press Club

THE OFFICE OF THE Golden Triangle Education Fund was located in the Old City, in a small building on a quiet street not far from the central police station. The other tenants were also nonprofits, including one making wheelchairs out of PVC pipe and bicycle tires, and another offering honorary elephant adoptions. Both worthwhile causes, Quinn thought, but maybe one organization was more grassroots than the other. The wheelchair group didn't offer free tote bags to donors.

The only other employee was Phen, Kay's young administrative assistant, a student at Chiang Mai University, majoring in international business. She had a few pink highlights in her sleek haircut, but otherwise she dressed for business, usually in a below-the-knee skirt and a crisp long-sleeved blouse. In addition to her facility with computer screens in both Thai and Roman scripts, she was adept at online publishing. As soon as Quinn got back from Baan Nakha, she offered to help design a brochure.

"You write the copy, and I'll get us a template," she said, already clicking keys on her computer.

"Great, Phen. Thanks."

Quinn hadn't felt such enthusiasm in years. He edited the brochure copy as meticulously as any brief he had ever written. After studying photo editing and colorization online, he strove to make the photographs from his trip, and more recent photos from Balmer showing progress, as engaging and attention grabbing as any in the *National Geographic*. He still remembered the piercing green eyes of the Afghan refugee girl on a cover in the 1980s.

The office was so small, Phen worked at the main desk and Quinn at a smaller one jammed into an alcove under the stairs that led to Kay's office. One afternoon in early November around five, Kay hollered down, "Hey, Jack, how about a beer?"

That was new.

"What?" he asked. Kay had seemed pleased with Quinn's newfound energy, but he wanted to make sure he'd heard correctly.

"A beer."

"Sounds good," he shouted back. "Where to?" he asked when Kay came downstairs.

"The Press Club, just down the street."

"Care to join us?' Quinn asked Phen.

"Thanks, *Khun* Jack. I have a meeting tonight."

The proprietor of the Press Club was a paunchy older Brit named Derek Davies. He had been a correspondent for the *Far Eastern Economic Review*, a weekly news magazine published in Hong Kong, now defunct. Derek had covered it all, from Vietnam to the killing fields of Cambodia, from the end of China's Cultural Revolution to the return of Hong Kong to the mainland.

When he retired, Derek had wanted to establish a hangout in Chiang Mai like the Continental Bar in Saigon—a place for, as he put it, "the usual lot of war correspondents, spies, political intriguers, thieves, bribers, and war groupies, which there always are."

Quinn had never been to Saigon but thought Derek had probably pretty much realized his vision. The long, narrow space had a carved teak bar backed by bottles of gin, bourbon, scotch, and Drambuie; Quinn had spotted a dusty bottle of Pimm's on the top shelf. The denizens were the expected mix of mostly British and American geezers, but some local university students came by, as did occasional backpackers and tourists directed there by one of the guidebooks that called the place "quirky."

Derek might be a bit of an intriguer himself, Quinn figured. Behind the bar hung a poster of Aung San Suu Kyi, leader of Burma's National League for Democracy Party, which was fighting for political reform against the military junta in Rangoon. She had been under house arrest for years.

Derek was behind the bar when Quinn and Kay entered. In his seventies, most likely—it was always hard to tell with aging, splotchy Europeans—he always wore bright red suspenders to hold up his trousers and kept his readers on a string. Derek was famous for his long puns and was unraveling one for an unsuspecting tourist couple. Something about the sand of one hound crapping. Derek had a million of them.

"Welcome, Kay," he roared. Derek either bellowed or spoke sotto voce, depending on the circumstance. As they took seats at the bar, he put down a bowl of macadamia nuts.

"And who's this gentleman, Kay?" Though he knew Jack well, he'd never been in with Kay before.

"Jack Quinn. He's working with the foundation."

Derek hung out a meaty paw and said, "Welcome, Quinn! First drink's on the house!"

Kay ordered an Old Fashioned; Quinn, a pint of Guinness. The ersatz Irish pubs in town served it with ice, but Derek, who called it "the black stuff," knew it was properly served at room temperature with a full head of foam. He brought Kay extra cherries.

As Derek served the drinks, he said to Quinn, switching to sotto voce, "Teddy Dingle was in here looking for you."

The Press Club hosted weekly trivia nights like the Gymkhana Club did, and sometimes Quinn and Teddy teamed up there too. A competition was scheduled for that night.

"Bit off-putting, that Dingle," Derek went on. "He knows his odd bits, but people find him obnoxious."

"Tell me about it."

"I heard he put the finger on young Tee at the club for the queen's-head business."

"You know Tee?" Derek seemed to know everybody.

"He comes in here once in a while. I haven't seen him lately."

Kay nodded as if to affirm that.

"Argues politics like college students are supposed to do. Smart kid. He told me I'm wrong about Aung San Suu Kyi, though. He said if she's ever released from house arrest, she'll make a Faustian bargain with the Burmese army to get them to share power. He says she doesn't care about the Rohingya, that Islamic group, or the hill tribes. I'm afraid he may prove right."

Derek moved toward the poster, where Aung San Suu Kyi was portrayed as Rosie the Riveter, arm muscles flexed and exhorting, "We can do it!" On the collar of her shirt was the fighting peacock of her National League for Democracy. Quinn thought he might be taking it down, but he was only straightening it.

"Never trust a politician," Kay said. "They always break your heart."

"Sounds kind of cynical," Quinn said.

"But almost always true," Derek said.

As the bar began filling with Happy Hour regulars, the noise level rose with the shouted greetings and the crash of the dice cups on the bar.

"Let's move," Kay said, picking up her drink, "to where it's quieter."

At the back of the club was a room furnished with over-stuffed chairs, lamps with good light, and racks of the latest editions of the *Guardian, Economist,* and *International Herald Tribune* newspapers. Recent issues of *Time* and the *New Statesman* magazines were jumbled on the tables in no particular order. Framed covers of the *Far Eastern Economic Review* hung on the wall.

When Quinn saw Teddy Dingle walk in, swiveling his neck like a barn owl, he was glad they had picked a table that was partly concealed from the bar. Teddy pushed his way through the crowd and demanded of Derek, who was pouring shots with both hands, "Have you seen Jack Quinn?"

Derek ignored him.

"Quinn, Jack Quinn, have you seen him lately?"

"Not lately," Derek answered without breaking his rhythm or telling a lie.

Teddy skulked off to the trivia table, where he found an Aussie who knew sports and recognized Teddy's savant-like memory for everything else. Every week, Derek came up with the questions and offered a free pitcher of beer to the winners. Now he asked the first one: Which ancient empire was conquered by the Romans in the fourth century?

"Etruscans," Teddy shouted.

"Good on you, mate," said his partner, who immediately stood Teddy a Carlsberg.

"Dodged a bullet," Quinn said as Teddy settled into the game.

"Good," said Kay. "You and I don't really get to talk that much. That's why I asked you to come out tonight."

Quinn wasn't sure that was true. Kay did a lot of talking, but it was mostly at him, it seemed.

"I've got to tell you, Jack," Kay said, "you're beginning to get some traction now. You started slow, but I'm liking what I'm seeing."

"What are you seeing?"

"New energy. Baan Nakha seems to have gotten you rolling."

"It's lucky we stumbled onto Roy Balmer."

"You're the one who took a chance and went up north with him. That's what I mean."

"Thanks."

"You're welcome. But you know, Jack, I'm still trying to figure out why you're here, considering what you left behind."

"I explained it to you, Kay. I needed a fresh start."

"We all need those, but why this exactly, building schools? In Thailand, for God's sake. I did see on your resume that you did some kind of relief work in Nicaragua when you were in college. Is there a connection?"

"Not really. I went to Managua to help clean up after the 1972 earthquake. My girlfriend was a member of the Catholic Newman Center at the University of Washington, and the priest was organizing a rescue mission. She was a starry-eyed idealist. I was starry-eyed too. Over her."

"Sometimes motives don't matter. It's the results that count."

"Maybe. Anyway, we went at Christmas break. By the time we got there, there were so many volunteers, we were tripping over each other. The radical priest…"

"Sorry?"

"The Jesuit who was our group leader. Preached liberation theology. He arranged for us to go into the northern highlands to a town called Jinotega. It was Sandinista country—rebels trying to topple their American-backed leader, Somoza, in a revolution. Remember that?"

"A little. Mostly I remember Iran-Contra."

"Right. Well, we helped with the coffee harvest. I wore a Che Guevara T-shirt."

"And so you got idealized and radicalized. Became a champion of the downtrodden."

"Maybe for a short time, I loved it. But the next year, after graduation, I went on to law school. I wanted to be a public defender or something like that. But four years later, the job market was tight. The only thing I could get was an associate position at an insurance company."

"Maybe you didn't look hard enough."

"Maybe. But I had student loans to pay, and I hired on with a big Seattle-based company, Safeco."

"I've heard of them. They have the ballpark."

"Right. So I moved up the ladder, from litigating individual claims to defending corporate cases. There was lots going on in my life. Got married—not to the Nicaragua girl—had two kids, established myself, made partner. By the time I was forty, I had a house in Laurelhurst and enough to pay cash for a thirty-six-foot sloop, the *Nolo Contendere*, to sail on Puget Sound.

"It was okay, in the beginning. But at some point, helping a big company avoid paying insurance claims became pure drudgery. Sometimes I didn't feel comfortable with the side I had to take. I'd lie awake at night not thinking about whether I'd lose a case but what I had to do to win. I lost whatever interest I ever had in the work, and that led to losing interest in pretty much everything else."

"Poor thing."

"Yeah, right? But I hated the constant conflict, having to deal with lots of assholes, and especially questioning my own integrity nearly every day."

"Isn't that what lawyers do?"

"Some of them. Not all."

"You should've done some pro bono work."

"I did. Lots."

"I still don't get it. Lots of people go through crises like that without blowing everything up."

"A year and a half ago, my wife asked for a divorce. She got tired of seeing me lying on the couch watching the Huskies and Sonics and making no effort to do things she was interested in, like going to an art exhibition or a play. My daughters blame me."

"Sounds like maybe they should."

"If you're looking for someone to blame, I guess. And my performance at work began to fall off. I missed a couple of filing dates, something a competent lawyer never does."

"So you lost your job?"

"Not exactly. I'd been there a long time, done good work. The other partners 'suggested' I take six months to a year off. Kind of like a sabbatical. They'd keep me on at half pay, and either I'd straighten up or I was gone."

"Did you get any professional help?"

"Only long enough to get a prescription for Prozac. Still waiting for it to kick in."

"And so here you are. But why here exactly? Why come to Thailand?"

"Like I told you. I wanted something completely different. Different work, different setting. And maybe you're right, I was looking for something that made me feel as good as Nicaragua did."

"You can't go home again."

"Maybe not. But as you said, here I am. Which leads me to a question. Why did you hire me in the first place?"

"It wasn't the first place. Picked a young woman from Berkeley. But at the last minute, she got a graduate school offer that was too good to turn down. We were left hanging. You were available."

"Strong vote of confidence."

"Don't go and get your feelings hurt. You said you had a treasure trove of contacts with money, and you had some legal skills we could use. You got us our 501c3, for tax deductibility in the States. That was big. And we figured you wouldn't need much hand holding. You're not a kid."

"That's for sure."

They changed the subject by moving back to the bar, where the trivia players were still shouting answers. Two young tourists, one sporting a straw fedora and the other in a cotton sarong, probably both just purchased at the night market, strolled in. The guy ordered a mojito.

"I can give you a shot or a beer," Derek said. "We don't muddle."

"Dive bar," the guy confided to his companion.

Derek's hearing was still acute, even if his pace was slow.

"Absolutely correct, lad. Not your sort of establishment at all. Might I recommend one of those trendy new places on Nimanhaemin Road? Try the Monkey Club. Roof-top bar, flowery drinks, music every night. I hear Dengue Fever is in town. Ever hear of them? Best Cambodian surfer band in the world."

"Thanks, man. How do we get there?"

Derek came from behind the bar, put his hand on the young man's shoulder, and not that gently guided him to the door. He pointed north down Si Puhm Road.

"Walk that way for about a mile. Turn left on Niman-haemin. You can't miss it."

"You sent them the wrong way, Derek," Kay said when he returned to the bar.

"Did I now?"

During the day, Derek preferred to play classical music: Debussy, Ravel, Vivaldi. Or the cool jazz of Dave Brubeck and early Miles later in the afternoon. But at Happy Hour, the patrons demanded oldies. And as the evenings progressed and the crowd's exuberance increased, they wanted something they could dance to. Derek had reluctantly installed a small parquet dance floor and a disco ball.

Now it was the Beach Boys ("I Get Around"), Creedence ("Run Through the Jungle"), and the Contours' "Do You Love Me (Now That I Can Dance)."

A regular Kay knew came up. "How about it, Kay?" he asked, nodding his head toward the dance floor.

"Maybe later, Jerry," she said.

Quinn and Kay stayed until the trivia match was over. Teddy and his mate won. When he collected his pitcher of beer, he hoisted it in Quinn's direction. He didn't offer to share.

CHAPTER SEVEN

Progress in Baan Nakha

THE REPORTS FROM BAAN Nakha continued to look encouraging, but Quinn couldn't help thinking an on-site visit was in order. Kay agreed.

"You need to look in on Tee too," she said.

"Come on up," Balmer told him. "We have plenty to show you."

So in mid-November, Quinn was back on the bus to Fang. Balmer met him at the station on the Superhawk. After giving him a bear hug and a "good to see you, bro," he took Quinn's duffel and threw it into the trailer.

The ride to the village seemed far shorter than on the first trip, despite the fact that sitting on the pillion for an hour was not something Quinn relished. He held onto the seat and balanced the best he could.

On entering the village, he noticed a lashed-together wooden structure that looked something like a giant swing.

"What is that?" he asked Balmer over the quiet idling of the slow-moving motorcycle.

Balmer answered out the side of his mouth, keeping his eyes on the rough road.

"It's the wedding swing," he said. "The Akha have a festival at the end of the harvest to pray for a good crop in the coming year. It's also a coming-out party for girls approaching marriage age."

"Tee better watch out," said Quinn.

"He's safe, I think. The festival will start in about a week. The shaman is figuring out the most propitious date." Preparations for the festival had begun in earnest. The women were gathered outside the houses trying on the traditional clothing they had been working on all year: indigo-dyed cotton jackets and leg wrappings embroidered in light blue, dark green, yellow, and gold. Quinn admired the ornate headgear, decorated with beads, silver balls, feathers, tassels, and ancient coins.

When Tee spotted Balmer and Quinn, he climbed down from the schoolhouse's new metal roof. As always, greetings included a *wai*, then a handshake. Quinn draped an arm around Tee's shoulder.

"Great seeing you, Tee," he said. "How's it going?"

"This is turning out not to be punishment after all, *Kuhn* Jack. Clean air, hard work; I'm loving it." Tee showed him the hard new callouses on his hands. "And the people are really great."

"That's what I'm hearing."

Tee snagged Quinn's bag from the trailer and led him into the building. The dormitory had been completed, and he and Balmer had set up there, with makeshift bunks for their sleeping bags and two camp chairs. The shop table had been repurposed as a desk and repository for their books.

"Where do you eat?"

"We eat with the villagers. We're their guests, they wouldn't have it any other way."

"How's the food?"

"The barking deer's a little gamey," Balmer said.

"Let us show you around."

Tee was obviously proud of the work they had accomplished. He led Quinn into the dorm bathroom and flushed a toilet. The water whooshed away. He turned a tap on the sink, and the water flowed strongly.

"Usually don't need hot," he explained. "But when it's cold, we can hook up the propane tank."

"How do you get the pressure?" Quinn asked. He hadn't seen a water-tank tower anywhere.

"We'll show you," said Balmer. "I see you brought your hiking shoes."

Quinn gave a thumbs up and looked down at his stylish new low-tops, bought specially for the trip.

"*Vamanos*, then," Balmer said.

He led them around to the side of the building, where a freshly dug trench held big PVC pipe that led straight up the mountainside for about five hundred feet. They huffed and puffed their way up a narrow trail until they reached a fast-flowing river that had been slightly diverted to feed the pipe.

"Fifty PSI at the tap," Balmer said proudly. "The river runs year-round. The only problem is sometimes a fish shows up in the toilet bowl."

"Genius," Quinn said.

"Sometimes the simplest solutions are the best."

Quinn noted the neat joinery of the sections of six-foot-long pipe.

"Tee," Balmer offered. "Hands of a surgeon."

"Check out the view," Tee said, leading them off the trail to a sweeping vista of the valley below. Except for patches of low-hanging fog and wisps of smoke from cooking fires, the view was clear for miles.

Back on the trail and falling into single file behind Balmer and Tee, Quinn asked about snakes.

"Occasional pit viper," Balmer said.

Quinn stopped short.

"Just kidding, Jack," said Balmer, but he swept the path with his walking stick as if he were checking for landmines.

It was quiet except for the sound of the gurgling river.

"Peaceful," Quinn said as they slowly descended the slope.

"Just like I like it," said Balmer. "Tee's beginning to hike the mountains too."

"Yup." Tee looked at his worn-in Blundstones and kicked some dirt off. He checked Quinn's hikers too. "*Kuhn* Roy says hiking can be like meditation. Make it a passive experience. Be mindful, step by step; let the trail come to you."

"Does that work for you?"

"It's beginning to."

They walked on for a while in silence. Then Quinn said to Tee, "Tell me about the swing ceremony."

"From what the teachers tell me, the celebration goes on for days. Music, singing, lots of food and drinks. Tug-of-wars."

"Do they participate?"

"Peu and Koh? The teachers?"

"Yes."

"No. They say they're too old. Which is kind of a joke with them. They're only in their twenties."

"*Kuhn* Roy says you'd better be careful with them."

"No worries. I'm not ready for marriage. I still have to fig-ure out what I'm doing. But I could do worse than getting my teaching certificate and coming back here. There are government programs now for rural schools."

"What would your parents think?"

"About my teaching or marrying an Akha girl?"

"Both."

"They'd be fine with my being a teacher here, very presti-gious. They're mostly worried about my moving to Bangkok. Politics scares them."

"They're smart," Balmer said from his position as point man, not taking his eyes off the trail.

They were halfway down the slope. The conversation continued in time with their careful steps.

"And the problem wouldn't be with my parents anyway,"

Tee continued. "It would be with the Akha. They tend to be clannish. They don't trust outsiders."

"With good reason," Balmer said. "Their way of life is on the endangered-species list. But they like you."

"True enough. They seem to be accepting me."

"While they've never seen anything like me," said Balmer. "They think I may be a ghost. Someone hung chicken feathers over my bunk once. But they're hospitable enough."

"Peu is super smart and funny," Tee said.

"To say nothing of being cute as a button," added Balmer.

"That too."

"When I was your age," Quinn said, cringing at the cliché, "I was in Nicaragua doing relief work with my girlfriend. I felt I could stay in that village with her forever."

"But you didn't."

"The new semester was starting, which I guess says something about the level of my commitment. But I often wonder how long our idealism would have lasted there."

"Maybe forever," Tee said.

"But probably not."

Tee shrugged. Balmer didn't seem to be listening.

As they reached the school site, Quinn could see the villagers streaming into the communal dining hall for dinner.

"I told them we'd be having a special guest," Balmer said.

The village headman, the *dzoema*, had reserved a place for Quinn next to him.

"This is a special feast," Balmer whispered. "In your honor. Both pork and chicken." Quinn looked for fish but saw none.

Tee ate with the teachers, although men and women generally ate separately. "What do the villagers think about that?" Quinn asked Balmer.

"They're not so crazy about it, but they're okay. They know the old ways are slipping away."

After sweet pumpkin pie and many toasts of the bitter rice

whisky that smelled like kerosene and set your mouth on fire, Quinn and Balmer staggered to the dormitory. Tee was already there, reading by headlight.

"Not Abraham Lincoln, but close," Quinn said to him.

"Almost a log cabin," Tee answered without looking up.

"What's the book?"

"More political theory. Greeks and Romans and their influence on American democracy. This chapter is about James Madison and the separation of powers. That's a good idea."

"Not enough of that here in Thailand?"

"Not by a long shot. You know the military is in control. We need a new constitution with political freedoms. Fair elections, some checks on royal power. That's what the demonstrations are all about."

Balmer opened *The Asian Journal.* "Ever read Merton, Jack?" he asked.

"I tried *The Seven Storey Mountain* in college. I wasn't sure about the one true church thing. I didn't get very far."

"You're a Catholic?"

"Was, I guess. Like everybody, I hung on until reason trumped the magical thinking."

"Me too. But Merton changed his tune over time. He began talking about syncretism, saying all religions have pretty much the same moral basis—to love one another, to be charitable. He thought that Christianity and Buddhism pretty much run on parallel tracks. The Ten Commandments and the Four Boundless Qualities—lots of overlap there."

"So the Baptist missionaries didn't need to come here."

"We didn't need to be saved," Tee said forcefully. "We already were."

"Same same but different," Balmer added.

CHAPTER EIGHT

Christmas in Chiang Mai

O NE MORNING IN MID-DECEMBER, Balmer called the foundation office on the sat phone. Kay picked up. "Hello, Roy, just a minute." She called down to Quinn. "Jack, pick up, it's Roy." And then "Everything okay up there, Roy?"

"Everything's copacetic, Kay. Should be finished by New Years. Only problem is it keeps getting colder. Takes days for the paint to dry."

"It's the same here," Kay said. "The weather reports say we could have snow on Doi Suthep soon. Can you imagine a white Christmas in Chiang Mai?"

"I can believe it. Weather is screwy all over the world. We're living in strange times, that's for sure. Which brings me to another thing we need."

"We're pretty much budgeted out, Roy. It's the end of the fiscal year. No room for big expenditures now."

"Don't worry, it's a little ask. It's the cold. We need blankets. It hit freezing last night, and the old folks and little ones are not doing well. They're not used to this."

"Warm blankets may be hard to find in Chiang Mai, Roy. Usually no need."

"Can you check around, maybe try Alibaba or something?"

"Sure. But how about this? Maybe we can do a blanket drive at the Gymkhana Club. The Christmas party is in a couple of weeks, and expats tend to pack heavy. There's

71

probably lots of blankets shoved into drawers and cupboards that've never been used."

"Sounds like it might be worth a try."

"I'll call Sarah Purcell. You know her, Jack. The Major's wife. Heads up the events committee."

"I don't think so," Quinn answered.

"Sure you do. She did the spring jumble sale. Great organizer. Anyway, Roy, I'll call her."

"Much appreciated."

Sarah Purcell ran the idea past the Christmas party subcommittee, where it met with quick approval.

"You know we like to do our part," she said on a return call to Kay. "Always have done."

The Major then sent out an e-blast promising a free mug of mulled wine for every blanket donated.

THE RUN-UP TO Christmas in Chiang Mai left Quinn feeling disoriented. Every bar and restaurant in town had a Merry Xmas sign in the window, with a holly wreath or frosted snow or both. The Khad Suan Kaew shopping plaza was decked out in Christmas trees decorated with strings of light and ornaments and featured a rotating, ho-ho-hoing Santa ten feet tall. Wherever you went, "Rudolph the Red-Nosed Reindeer" blared in the background.

Kay explained to Quinn that it was all just *sanuk*, fun, just another opportunity to celebrate an occasion with gifts and parties. No Baby Jesus required. Still and all, Quinn remained perplexed by the notion of fir trees and fake snow, not to mention a Laplander in a red suit with fur trim, in the tropics.

On the Wednesday before Christmas, Quinn stopped by the Gymkhana Club to check on progress with the blanket drive. The donation barrel in the foyer was filling up nicely with new and lightly used woolens and plush polyesters;

there was even a fringed tartan Burberry.

Sarah Purcell saw Quinn as he entered the dining room and beckoned him over. The decorations committee was busy setting up the Christmas crèche. Surrounded by barnyard animals, Saint Joseph doted over Mother Mary and the Christ child, but there seemed to be some disagreement over the Magi. Betsy Carstairs had placed them too close to the crib for Emma Boothroyd's sensibilities.

"They came from afar," Mrs. Boothroyd insisted.

"Very well," said Mrs. Carstairs, moving the wise men so close to the edge of the display table they were in danger of falling off. "Now they're in Syria," she said. "Is that far enough for you?"

Sarah Purcell cupped Quinn's elbow and led him away.

"Kay has filled me in about the Akha project you and Mr. Balmer are working on. And your helping young Tuanthon out of his little jam with work there. We're awfully fond of young Tee, you know. He's a fine young man. Could he and your man in Baan Nakha both come down for the party? We'd love to see them, and the Major would like to make the blanket presentation part of the formal program."

"I'm sure they'd be delighted." Quinn never used the word "delighted."

"Marvelous. Oh, if you'll excuse me." There was another dustup in Bethlehem.

Quinn called Balmer when he got back to the office.

"We've got blankets, Roy," he said. "They want you and Tee to accept them at the Christmas party. Can you make it?"

"Is the Pope Catholic?"

"Last time I checked. You can stay at my place."

"Mighty neighborly of you, Jack."

The day before the Christmas party, Quinn met Balmer and Tee at the bus station. Balmer had exchanged his cargo shorts for shiny black trousers. With them he wore a maroon dress shirt, poorly tailored but crisply ironed. His brown oxfords were freshly polished.

"Stopped in Fang to get my party duds," he said. "Want to make a good first impression."

Tee was right behind him. He had changed back to his trainers and T-shirt and was fidgeting. *Wais* and greetings were brief. Quinn knew he was anxious to get home.

"You're on your own, Tee. Just be at the club tomorrow at five o'clock. Give your parents my best."

Tee looked relieved. "Thanks, *Khun* Jack," he said as he took off. "See you tomorrow."

Quinn and Balmer proceeded to the Damn Rat. Quinn had done some light cleaning, throwing old newspapers away and plumping the sofa cushions. He wanted to be a good host. He had bought soft drinks and a jumbo bag of Ruffles at the 7-Eleven. And a six-pack of Singha in cans.

Balmer threw his bag on the couch and kicked off his shoes. He turned on Quinn's television and started flipping between CNN and a delayed-broadcast Rams game as if he'd always lived there. Quinn grabbed the chips and a beer from the kitchen and called Kay.

"They're here," he said.

"Can't wait to see them both. How does Tee seem?"

"Happy to be home. Is that 'Silent Night' I hear in the background?"

"I'm at the club, practicing with the chorus. We're going to do caroling on the Leonowens Verandah. Can you sing?"

"Soprano in the Saint Joe's boys' choir in Seattle until my voice changed."

"You were a choir boy?"

"Go figure."

"I'll count you in, then." Quinn didn't say no.

The festivities were set to start with a "no-host mingle" in the bar. Major Purcell met Quinn and Balmer at the door.

Decked out in his dress blues, with a crimson sash and a chest full of medals, he proffered each a snappy salute.

"Happy Christmas," the ruddy-faced Major roared to Quinn. And turning his attention to Balmer, he said, "And you, sir, must be the man of the hour. We've heard about your good work in the mountains. Terrible thing, being cold." He pointed to a blue-and-white battle ribbon. "I know. This one's for the Falklands."

"Thank you, sir," Balmer said quietly, reverting to the always slightly on-edge demeanor of an enlisted man in the presence of brass.

"Call me Purcell. We don't stand on ceremony around here. Right, Quinn?"

"Never."

"Well, do come in. Socialize a bit, have a drink, and enjoy our holiday feast. We'll do the blanket presentation after we eat dinner."

"Very good, sir," Balmer said, offering a twisted-finger attempt at a salute.

Tchaikovsky's *Nutcracker Suite* was playing as they entered the dining room. Perfect, Quinn thought. The electric fire in the corner, with stockings hung on a faux mantelpiece, was going full blast to fend off the chilly evening.

Kay, wearing a cocked elf's hat with jingle bells, waved and came over. Before Quinn could introduce Balmer, she said, "Great to finally meet you, Roy. I'm Kay."

"I know. Thank you, Kay. Thanks for taking a chance on me."

"Give Jack the credit. He believed in you, and so do I."

Quinn might have winced at that before but didn't now.

"How about a glass of champagne?" she asked.

"A small one, maybe," said Balmer.

"Of course."

Kay went to the bar, got a bottle of Australian bubbly

from the fridge, and grabbed an ice bucket.

"Right this way, gentlemen," she said, leading them to a table up front. Place cards with the names in elaborate calligraphy were tented round the table.

Quinn recognized all the names except one. "Who's Angun Mongpet?" he asked.

"That's Noi. From Sweetie Pie." Quinn didn't know her real name. Everyone he knew in Thailand had a nickname, it seemed.

As they sat down, Quinn asked, "Is Daryl coming?" He hadn't seen Kay's husband anywhere, although that was nothing new.

"Maybe later. He's working late at the airport again. Checking airplane tail numbers or something. I don't know."

A few minutes later, Tee arrived to a smattering of applause, "Here here," and "Welcome home" from the partygoers. Kay beamed, Balmer pulled out a chair, and Quinn poured him a glass of champagne.

From the edge of the crowd, Teddy Dingle sidled over. He noted the place cards, didn't see one for him, and sat down anyway.

"Places are reserved, Teddy," Kay said.

"Won't be but a minute. Just wanted to say hello. You must be the school-building chap," Teddy said to Balmer.

"What if I am?"

"He knows all about you," Quinn told him.

Teddy turned to Tee. "Sorry for the misunderstanding, young man. I just wanted you to get a good talking to, you know. Get you back on the straight-and-narrow. Respect for law-and-order and all that. All forgiven?"

"Nothing to forgive, Teddy," Tee responded, still sitting. He dispensed with the *Kuhn* and didn't call him Mr. Dingle. "You actually did me a favor," he went on. "I've had lots of time to read. I'm deep into Western political thought right now."

"Good lad. That's the ticket. Can't go wrong there."

"I'm studying world revolution too. You know, Trotsky and Marx, Mao and Uncle Ho."

"Indeed."

Teddy shot a glance at Quinn that could have meant "I told you so."

Tee wasn't done with Teddy. "You're just lucky I didn't put a Phi curse on you. Salt and chilies cooked in a black pot to make you itch all over."

"You could do that?"

"Of course not."

"I think I see Daryl," Kay said to Teddy. "Time for you to go." Daryl wasn't anywhere in sight.

"Why'd you let him sit down in the first place?" Quinn asked Kay after Teddy scuttled off.

"I guess I'm just a sucker for the possibility of redemption. Thought he might recognize the error of his ways and thoroughly apologize."

"Maybe next time around," Balmer said.

"Gam," Tee sighed. "The dude's got bad karma."

The Major, now at his place on the dais, stood up and tinkled a water glass with a butter knife. As the crowd settled down, he announced that dinner was served.

"Those at Table One first, if you please, followed by the rest of you in numerical order. Check your number."

Kay led off, followed by Quinn, then Balmer after doing a brief Alphonse-and-Gaston routine. Tee came after his elders, and Teddy tagged along, giving an "I'm with them" look to the mildly peeved onlookers. The rest of the diners fell in behind, and the music switched to perennial favorites: "White Christmas," "O Little Town of Bethlehem," "Silent Night."

The long buffet tables were laden with turkeys, roast beef, glazed ham, scalloped potatoes, salmon mousse, and roasted vegetables. An assortment of Noi's fresh-baked pies and cakes was on a table by the coffee and hot-water urns.

After a roistering hour of bonhomie, seconds, and, in some cases, third servings, the club's wait staff began to clear the tables. The Major cut off the music and rose to speak. First, he acknowledged all those who had made the event a success, "better this year than ever." That included the dining room staff, all of whom had put in overtime, and the decorations committee, which, in addition to setting up the nativity scene, had strung the colored lights and decorated the tree.

"I hope I haven't forgotten anyone," the Major said. He pulled a list from a jacket pocket and double-checked. Satisfied, he paused a moment for dramatic effect. "And now, dear friends, this year at the Gymkhana Club, we have a special way of showing the true meaning of Christmas. By that, I mean the joy of giving."

He signaled fellow club officers to wheel carts stacked with blankets from the back of the room up front.

"There's nothing worse than being cold," the Major repeated. "And thanks to your generosity, the people of the village of Baan Nakha will be sleeping better tomorrow night. Kay Kerwin, Jack Quinn, and Roy Balmer of the Golden Triangle Education Fund and our own Tuantong Boonprasan, we salute you for the good work you're doing for our friends in the mountains." And he saluted them, briskly, to ringing acclamation from the partygoers.

After the Major's remarks, the crowd gathered out on the Leonowens Verandah for the caroling. The women donned bonnets, and some of the men wore bowlers or top hats. A *papier mâché* streetlamp meant to evoke a Victorian Christmas added to the feeling of nostalgia.

The chorus director, a woman Quinn had never seen, started every song with a tweet on her pitch pipe. Knowing that Quinn and Kay and Balmer would not know the words to British standards like "Once in Royal David's City" and "Holly and Ivy," Sarah Purcell had handed them songbooks with the lyrics. "No Rudolph," she had forewarned.

Caroling done, leftovers boxed, the celebration began to wind down about nine. The Major took to the microphone once again.

"I just got a notice on the weather app," he announced, looking at his cell phone. "It's snowing on Doi Suthep! A white Christmas in Chiang Mai. Can you believe it? What are the odds of that?" He added a warning to drive safely, as if blizzard conditions had set in, and bade them all another "Happy holidays!"

"Let's see if we can spot the snow on the mountain," Quinn said to no one in particular. Many of those still remaining trooped back out to the Leonowens Verandah. Quinn was pretty sure he could see the dark, white-tipped peak of Doi Suthep in the near distance. Kay thought she could too.

Balmer looked up into the clear sky. "Look. The North Star," he said softly.

CHAPTER NINE

The Veterans

EARLY IN THE NEW YEAR, celebrated with fireworks and floating sky lanterns over the River Ping, Balmer telephoned Quinn. The villagers were warm in their new blankets, he reported, and they were putting the finishing touches on the new school. He was riding the Superhawk down to Chiang Mai to pick up Halogen light bulbs for the classrooms, he told Quinn. He needed the 6500 Kelvin blue hue, which was supposed to be best for student concentration during math.

"How long are you staying?" Quinn asked.

"Just overnight."

"Okay. Stay with me."

"I was hoping you might say that."

Balmer must have left the village at the crack of dawn, because Quinn heard the blat of the motorcycle in the car park just past ten. He hustled out of his apartment and took the stairs two at a time.

"I thought Hondas were supposed to be quiet," he said to Balmer. "Yours sounds like a Harley."

"Free-flow exhausts. Adds power on the top end."

Balmer revved the engine several times to demonstrate and then let it return to idle. The angry noise brought neighbors to their windows.

"Nice. Park it over there. You're leaking oil."

Balmer wheeled the bike to the shade of a palmetto tree

and pulled his rucksack out of a saddle bag. Once in Quinn's apartment, he dropped the bag on the couch and said, "How about breakfast?" He looked at his watch. "Or lunch."

"Got just the place. Let me call Kay to see if she wants to join us. Morning, Kay," Quinn said as soon as she answered. "Roy's in town," which would explain why he wasn't at the office yet. "Join us for lunch? Sweetie Pie?"

"Love to, but there's a bit of a dustup on the home front, I'm afraid."

"Daryl being a jerk again?"

"Something like that. Hey, I've got to go. Lunch is on me. Say hi to Roy. And to Noi."

"Roger that." That's what Quinn figured Daryl might say over radio chatter during his surveillance operations out at the airport.

"Kay says hi," Quinn told Balmer. "She can't join us. Ready to eat?"

"What's Sweetie Pie?"

"Best American food in town. You remember Noi from the Christmas party. She owns the place."

"She was at our table."

"Right. Her place is across town. Tuk-tuk distance."

"Why waste the *baht*? We can take the bike."

Balmer was fine on the highway, but Quinn wondered how he would handle the helter-skelter of Chiang Mai city traffic. Once more, Balmer surprised him. Finessing the roundabouts, he seemed to sense the traffic around them as he dodged the buses, other bikes, and tuk-tuks.

Quinn directed Balmer down Nimanhaemin Road, pointing out Sweetie Pie's bright pink awning in the middle of the block. Balmer parked on the sidewalk, like everyone else. After negotiating the tangle of motorbikes, stepping sideways, and sucking in their guts, they traversed the last few yards to the door.

The menu was in the window. Balmer scanned it and asked Quinn, "What's good?" Before Quinn could tell him, he stopped short. "Wait. What the fuck is that?" he shouted. The toe of his boot was pointing to an American POW-MIA decal on the door, the one with the drooping silhouette of a prisoner of war surrounded by barbed wire with a guard tower.

"The VFW meets here every month."

"There's a fucking VFW post in Chiang Mai?"

"How did you not know that?"

"I don't do vets."

"Lots of them retired here after the Vietnam War."

"That much I know. But what's with this goddamned 'missing in action' bullshit? There are no more Vietnam prisoners of war, and the only ones missing are the guys who were so strung out on heroin at the end of their tours, they skipped their flights home. If anyone's concerned about missing Americans, they don't have to look very far. Like the Bui Doi, dust children, the kids left behind by their G.I. dads. Thousands of them. They're easy to find. They're not hiding. This is bullshit."

"What about the dead MIAs?"

"They're dead."

Quinn was caught off guard. He had not witnessed Balmer's flashing anger before, and this was explosive. He wondered what had set him off.

"We can find somewhere else to eat," Quinn offered. "There's a Sizzler up the street."

"Hell, no. I want to eat here. I want to meet these assholes." He was already swinging the front door open with sufficient force to bang the stop. "Any of these VFW motherfuckers here today, do you think?"

"Maybe." Quinn knew that it was more than likely.

Balmer took several deep, cleansing breaths, eyes closed

and palms up. He completed his centering routine with a nod, and they walked into Sweetie Pie.

The smell of strong coffee mingled with the aroma of freshly baked breads and pastries. As usual, Noi, her apron splotched with flour, was taking orders at the counter.

"Hi, guys!" she shouted over the hubbub of the lunch rush. "Sit anywhere."

"By the window?" Quinn suggested. His usual table was being vacated, but the remains of Eggs Benedict and waffles soggy with syrup remained. He quickly cleared it.

Balmer scanned the restaurant. "Is that them?" he asked, nodding toward a large circular table in the back, with a big Reserved sign and occupied by three older *farangs*.

"Could be."

It was. The vets were easy to spot. In some ways, they were still in uniform, with mesh baseball caps, white T-shirts showing under short-sleeved shirts; each favored knock-off-brand running shoes and black socks.

Balmer marched up to the table, where the vets sat oblivious to the incoming round. He startled them when he more demanded than asked, "Mind if we join you?"

"Always room for a brother," said one of the vets, who looked like a lifer with his high-and-tight buzz cut. Sticking out his hand for a shake, he introduced himself as Bill Smith. "Post commander," he clarified.

A grizzled old-timer, with blue and yellow inhalers parked on the table next to his smokes, shoved a chair back. "Master Sergeant Sweeney," he huffed.

"Army or Air Force?" asked the third vet, this one bean-pole skinny, with a twang that suggested Kentucky hollers.

Balmer seemed momentarily stymied. "Army" was all he could muster. The cordial welcome had caught him off guard. "Americal Division, Quang Tri Province," he added. "Sixty-eight to sixty-nine."

"Vietnam. Grunt."

"Yup."

"That must have been some shit," Beanpole said.

"Got that right. But I got winged by some shrapnel on a sweep through a ville. That was my ticket off the line. Got assigned to garrison duty at Long Binh."

"You were lucky."

"Except for Tet, yeah."

"Didn't see any of that," Bill Smith said. "We were all Air Force REMFs here in Thailand. At the airbase in Khorat, in the northeast. The mission was to bomb the shit out of Laos and the Ho Chi Minh Trail. Dumped tons of Agent Orange, so that you could see the NVA bastards trucking down the highway."

"We're paying a price, though," Beanpole told them. "Coming down with Parkinson's, lymphomas, brain cancer, and all kinda shit. We've lost a couple just recently. These guys jockeyed barrels of Agent Orange the shit onto bombers. If you served in Vietnam and get one of those diseases, the VA assumes it's from the exposure in the field, and they compensate you. If you served here, you have to prove you were exposed: when and where. They're not making it easy."

"Fucking bureaucrats," Master Sergeant Sweeney offered.

"You guys okay?" Quinn asked.

Sweeney said, "Sure, no problem."

Beanpole rapped the wooden table twice. "Where'd you serve?" he asked Quinn, who was hanging back.

"Didn't get the opportunity."

"No matter," Bill Smith said. "Join us anyway, as long as you're a friend of...?"

"Roy Balmer." He took the offered seat.

"First beer's on me, club protocol," said the commander. "It's close enough to noon. That's when we generally switch over from coffee."

Balmer hesitated, but Quinn jumped in to fill the gap. He tried to sound comradely. "Love to," he said and immediately realized that wasn't the thing to say.

Catching the eye of a server, Bill Smith covered his half-full coffee mug and held up five fingers.

Message received and translated, a waitress delivered five bottles of Singha ASAP. No glasses required.

Quinn and Balmer had come for lunch, and the encounter with the vets hadn't completely thrown them off track. Balmer scanned the blackboard specials and opted for the meatloaf.

"Lots of gravy," he told the waitress.

"Good choice," Quinn said and ordered the same. The vets weren't ready to eat yet.

Balmer dug into his meal. It wasn't until several minutes had passed, after taking a big bite of a Parker House roll, that he broached the subject.

"What's with the MIA sticker out front?"

"Oh, that," said Bill Smith. "That there's what you call operational bullshit. VFW headquarters in Kansas City," he pronounced it *Kanzity*, "says all posts have to put it up. SOP for everybody."

"That's Standard Operating Procedure," Balmer translated for Quinn.

"I know what it means."

"You're right, Roy. Nobody's missing here, last time I checked," Bill Smith said. "You guys missing anybody? All present and accounted for?"

Master Sergeant Sweeney took a drag on his half-smoked cigarette and followed up with a hit of Salbutamol, then hoiked a phlegmy cough. "The gang's all here," he said.

"We're good," said Beanpole.

Balmer swigged his beer and then put the bottle down. "Any G.I.s here leave their Thai kids behind? Like in Vietnam.

Any *bui doi*?"

"Sure. They call them *luk kreung* here. *Hapa*, like in Hawaiian, half-half. Some of those kids were treated bad after the war by the Thais, especially the Black ones. They saw them as an embarrassment. But things have changed. Seems like all the movie stars and singers and models are some *luk kreung* now. The kids like the European look."

During a pause on the cooking line, Noi came over to the table. "Had to say hello. Great seeing you again, Roy. How are the blankets working out?"

"Great. Still screwy weather, though."

"Just don't start talking about goddamned climate change," Master Sergeant Sweeney growled.

Noi ignored him. "Did I hear you guys talking about *luk kreung* just now?" she asked.

"I was," Balmer said. "Kids missing in action from the war."

"They're fine, Roy. I know one. Her name's Samorn, from Khorat, where I grew up."

"Where is she now?"

"Here. Chiang Mai. When the Americans left after the war, a lot of us moved here. And Roy, she's fine. Runs her own tour company, temples and elephants. Her dad was stationed at the base, and her mom worked at the bank. That sort of thing happened. It was almost fifty years ago. *Mai pen rai*, for God's sake. It doesn't matter anymore."

"Happens in every war," Bill Smith offered.

"Samorn says her dad stayed in touch for a while. Said he would bring them over to the States as soon as he could. But he was just a kid too. Memories are short. Things change. Life goes on."

A bell sounded from the kitchen.

"Pies are done," Noi said as she headed back to the kitchen.

And the conversation about *bui doi* and *luk kreung* was pretty much done too. For the time being, anyway, as far as the vets were concerned. They shifted back to more familiar territory, recalling the travails of keeping the planes flying.

"Hydraulics lines melted in the heat."

"Humidity corroded the airframes."

"Had to jury-rig everything."

"The F-4 was a total piece of crap."

"Heavy, slow, avionics always on the fritz."

"Give me a C-130 transport any day. Fat Albert. Couldn't bring that plane down for love nor money."

"Engine was easy to work on. Like a straight-six Chevy."

"Allison turbo prop. Made four thousand horsepower easy."

"Could fly in any weather."

And on and on. The vets were just warming up, like planes on the runway, waiting in line to take off with another yarn. Oft-told tales, exaggerations encouraged. Laughs and knee slaps guaranteed. Remember the times. Blowing the smart-ass lieutenant off the wing of his plane with a high-pressure fuel hose. "Sorry, sir!"

Three beers in, Balmer pushed his chair from the table.

"Where you going?" Bill Smith asked. "It's early."

"Have some work to do, fellas." He looked at Quinn, signaling it was time to go.

"Hold on a while." Bill Smith reached into a canvas briefcase he had stowed under the table. He scrounged among a bunch of papers and retrieved one.

"VFW Chiang Mai Central Post 5068 membership application," he said to Balmer. "Join us."

Balmer took the form.

"Think about it," Bill Smith said.

"Will do."

But Balmer didn't think on it very long. On the way out, he tossed the application into the nearest trash bin.

"Why did you go off like that on them about *bui doi*?" Quinn asked.

"Vets groups didn't do shit to bring those kids home after the war. Missing in action my ass."

"I don't get it."

"Figure it out."

"You left somebody behind."

"Thuong, Tommy, my son. His mother worked as a hooch girl at Long Binh. We were going to get married. You could do that if you jumped through enough hoops and after the chaplain tried to talk you out of it. They were going to join me in the U.S."

"What happened?"

"Didn't happen is more like it. I wrote, tried to arrange things. But not hard enough, I guess. All the red tape. Most Vietnamese didn't have birth certificates, although we got one for Thuong. I wrote and sent money for a year, got laid off from my construction job during a building slump. Etcetera, etcetera, and etcetera. Like Noi said, life went on. But I never forgot them when I was thinking straight."

"Did you ever try to find him after you lost track?"

"On and off. I'm sure they went back to his mother's village. I have no idea where that is. I learned about some internet sites trying to make matches with vets and their kids, but no luck for me."

Balmer pulled a shopping list from his shirt pocket. "Where do we get fucking light bulbs in this town?"

"DIY Center. Out in Lamphun."

The store was a big box, about the size of Loew's in the States. Balmer burst through the front door, almost taking out the employee passing out flyers with the weekly sales items. "Light bulbs!" he barked at the greeter, who pointed him in the general direction.

When he found the ones he needed, Balmer began filling up the hand basket Quinn had brought to him, thinking he might need it. Shopping didn't take long. In and out. At the self-checkout, Balmer scanned one, hit twelve, and gently placed the bulbs in the basket as if they were eggs. He handed them to Quinn.

"Be careful," he said. "They break easy."

As they approached the Superhawk, Quinn said, "What do you say we take the afternoon off, Roy? Catch a movie. The new Bond is in town."

But it was no use. "Gotta get back. I can be in Fang by dark if I leave now."

"You're not staying the night?"

"No."

They stopped at Quinn's apartment just long enough for Balmer to retrieve his bag and repack the light bulbs with crumpled newspaper. He bungeed the box to the passenger seat and drove off slowly, waving a hand without turning around.

CHAPTER TEN

Paduang

THE BAAN NAKHA SCHOOL project was completed in early January. Unseasonal, heavy rains had followed the cold spell in the mountains and further slowed the construction process. But the pictures Balmer attached to his weekly updates showed solid construction work, wiring that was neat, and spot welds that went beyond tradecraft and approached art.

"He's a master," Kay said to Quinn when he showed her the photos.

"He is," Quinn replied.

TEE WASTED NO TIME in returning to Chiang Mai when the school was done. Shortly after he returned, he called Quinn.

"I'm doing a shift at the club tonight."

"They let you back in?"

"With open arms. The Major said he might give me a raise, depending on how things go. Swing by tonight, I'll catch you up."

"Wouldn't miss it."

And neither would Kay. They got to the club at six, when Happy Hour was winding down and the dinner rush had yet to start.

Tee was behind the bar, slicing limes for gimlets and lemons for martinis. As soon as he saw them, he came around the bar and, forgoing the *wais*, gave them both hugs.

"You look good," Kay said, stepping back and giving him a quick once-over.

Quinn noticed that too. Some of the softness that had given Tee his boyish appearance had been replaced with a firmness that matured him.

"So what next, Tee?" Kay asked.

"I'll do one more semester at CMU and then transfer down to Bangkok in the fall. Thammasat University has a good international-relations program. Lots of analytics, visiting professors from everywhere, emphasis on the Pacific Basin."

"Maybe you'll be a senator someday," she told him.

"Stranger things have happened."

"Opposition party, I'm guessing," said Quinn.

"We'll have to wait and see." His smile hadn't changed.

"So no more school building for a while?"

"Not for me right now. I know *Khun* Roy's anxious for another project."

"We know," Quinn said, nodding.

Word about the success of the Baan Nakha project had begun to spread. It wasn't long before requests from other villages in the northeast began arriving at the GTEF office. Kay held up a letter from the Provincial Tribal Peoples Commission in Mae Hong Son, two hundred forty kilometers northwest of Chiang Mai on the Burmese border.

"This sounds good," she said. "The commission has off-the-shelf plans for a new school. Simple design, easy to build; they'll provide the materials. They want us to help with the construction. It's in a village called Na Soi. It's Paduang."

From Quinn's reading about Thailand's hill tribes—the Akha, Lahu, Mien, Hmong, Lisu, and Karen—he knew that the Paduang were a sub-group of the Karen. All the travel guides featured photographs of the women in the traditional brass coils that stretched the cervical vertebrae and compressed the ribcage to elongate the neck. Theories abounded as to the origin and purpose of this practice: from paying homage to an ancestral dragon spirit to protecting the women from being dragged into the jungle by tigers to sheer vanity. Some *farangs* called the Paduang "long necks" and arrived by the busload to gawk and take pictures to amaze their friends back home. Others called the practice barbaric. Some did both.

"We'd be working with the Paduang?" he asked.

"Do you any problem with that?"

"Nope, not a bit. Not if you don't."

"I don't."

"Done and done." Quinn was picking up the expat patois.

"We need to meet with the village leaders and scout the site," Kay added.

"When?"

"As soon as we can."

Quinn called Balmer in Fang, then waited through several rings for him to answer.

"Roy, this is Jack Quinn. What's going on?"

"Not much. Back in Fang. Cleaning tools, fixing the sander. The dog's glad to see me." Quinn heard a happy bark in the background.

"We've got another job. It's in Mae Hong Son Province. Interested?"

"Shit, yeah. I know Mae Hong Son like the back of my hand. I've done lots of work up there. When do we start?" he asked, echoing Quinn.

"Right away. Usual drill, though. We have to check out the site."

"Count me in."

"I think Kay might want to come along on this one."

"She'll like Mae Hong Son. Pretty little town on a lake."

"I'm going!" Kay shouted down from her office.

"It's a six-hour drive!" Quinn shouted back up. He didn't

want to discourage her from coming, but given a choice, he would have preferred traveling alone.

"No worries. We'll fly Nok Air, it's only a hundred bucks." Nok, the regional carrier, sported a yellow smiley-bird face across the nose of its 737s that made Quinn think of Southwest Airlines. "I'll firm up a date," she said.

A week later, Phen drove them to the airport in the foundation van for an afternoon flight. Daryl was on duty in his pickup truck, checking out the private planes as they landed. He was supposed to be incognito, even though the backwards Atlanta Braves baseball hat and the huge binoculars poking over the steering wheel pretty much blew his cover. Phen beeped as they drove past him, but Daryl didn't acknowledge the greeting. Kay didn't wave.

The Nok was fitted out for short runs. Quinn's knees banged up against the bulwark of the row in front of them.

"It's only an hour," Kay reassured him as she put in her earbuds. Quinn had the outside seat and dangled a leg in the aisle whenever he could.

Halfway through the short flight, she nudged him.

"Listen to this." She handed Quinn one of the buds, and their heads came together as they listened to the sounds of soft jazz.

"Who's that on the sax?" Quinn asked.

"King Bhumibol, the current king. This is 'Blue Day.' He composed it in the fifties. Herbie Hancock covered it."

Quinn had heard that the king was an internationally recognized jazz musician, but he'd never heard him play. He listened to the saxophone float up and dip gracefully back down and thought once again what an idiot Teddy Dingle was.

"Where are we staying?" Quinn asked as they descended the gangway to the tarmac.

"Grande View Hotel," Kay said. "It's on Nong Jong Lake. In

96

the center of town. It comes highly recommended; I checked with Noi's friend Samorn."

The Grande View was a boutique hotel appealing to the increasing numbers of package tourists exploring the Golden Triangle. It was a few rungs up from the funky hundred-*baht* hostels on Praphat Road young adventurers favored. When Kay checked in, the reception clerk handed her three keys.

"Thanks, boss."

"For what?"

"Not making me bunk with Roy."

"No problem. The feeling's probably mutual." She had a point, Quinn thought.

They rolled their carry-ons through the lobby and spotted Balmer settled in a plush lounge chair, his rucksack on the floor beside him. Deep into his bulky thriller, this one a Ludlum, he showed a quick startle response when Kay said hello.

"Sorry," he said.

"Sorry," Kay said. "Good to see you again, Roy." After a few pleasantries, she handed out their keys, then took the handle of her bag and started moving toward the elevator. "Let's meet at five for drinks on the terrace."

KAY HAD CHOSEN A table with an unobstructed view of Wat Jong Kham, on the far side of the lake. As they discussed logistics for the next day, the sun set on the tall, slender *chedi* of the temple, causing it to glow as if sheathed in gold. The surrounding mountains faded from bright to dark green and then to black. Gradually, the peaks disappeared altogether, their looming presence more felt than seen. A cold wind swept down from the heights and raised a chop on the lake.

"Inside?" Quinn suggested.

"Yes, please," Kay said, hugging her shoulders.

As they walked through the dining room toward an empty table, Quinn spotted something that caught his attention. "Who's Rambo?" he asked Balmer. A fortyish *farang*—shaved head, thick arms covered with tattoos, a sheathed combat knife strapped to his thigh—was talking to two kids, gym-buff and wearing camo gear that looked just bought. "Looks like Boy Scouts with a homicidal troop leader," Quinn observed.

"Not far off," Balmer responded. "I know him. Guy's named Jimmy Kruger. South African. He's one of the clowns around here playing at war in Burma. They try to hire on as mercenaries with the Karen army, but the Karen want nothing to do with them. They get in the way, stumble into ambushes, get caught and then cry to their embassies to save them. Total ass-hats. You'll usually find Kruger here in the bar telling kids made-up stories and trying to cadge a beer."

"You guys keep calling it Burma. I thought it was Myanmar now."

"That's what the junta wants you to call it. Supposedly less colonial. The full name is Republic of the Union of Myanmar. It's supposed to represent a unified country of many different peoples, which is obviously bullshit."

Balmer was building up a head of steam again. He went over to Kruger's table.

"Minding the nippers, Jimmy?" he asked.

"Fuck you, Balmer," Kruger responded.

"Don't listen to this jerk-off," Balmer said to the kids in camo, who seemed to be trying to decide who to take more seriously. "Go south to Koh Samui. Enjoy the beach. Get a massage. Have some fun. Just don't get involved in this shit."

Kruger started to rise from his chair. Balmer didn't flinch, and Kruger sat down again.

"Time to boogie," said one of the boys, taking his issue

of *Soldier of Fortune* magazine with him. The other followed, looking over his shoulder at what had just transpired.

Kay started moving toward a table on the other side of the room. "How do you know that guy?" she asked Balmer.

"It's like I told Jack. I've done lots of work in the area. I keep tripping over him."

"But you've never done any work with him?" Kay emphasized the word "work."

"Of course not. You can't be around here without knowing what's going on is all."

THE NEXT MORNING, THEY met their counterparts in the hotel lobby. *Khun* Praew was a thirtyish young man wearing a Royalist yellow polo emblazoned with the logo of the National Refugee Resettlement Commission. *Khun* Ananda, a tight-lipped young woman with a ponytail, in jeans and a white blouse, was from the Provincial Education Board. All loaded onto a government van freshly washed for the journey. Water was still dripping from the door rails.

As they set off, Balmer, from his seat in the back of the van, shouted, "I know a short cut." The driver looked at *Khun* Praew for guidance. He nodded.

It was a short drive to the village of Na Soi, less than ten miles Balmer's way, the last few down a dirt road that heavy truck tracks had scarred and left deeply rutted. What Balmer had failed to mention was that actually reaching the village required fording a river at the road's end. The driver, after shooting a look at Balmer in the rear-view mirror, parked at the edge.

Balmer ahoyed a group of villagers on the other side, who launched three small boats and poled over. The delegation gingerly boarded the tippy craft and were offered helping hands by the welcoming committee when they disembarked.

The village headman, flecks of gray in his hair and showing signs of impending portliness, introduced himself as Hawhne Shwe. He had the smiling, affable, how-the-heck-are-you demeanor of a mayor from a small town anywhere in the world.

Hawhne Shwe led the group up a short rise to the village's main street, already filled with early-morning tourists. The Paduang women, coils on their necks and in colorful traditional clothing, were posing for pictures. Signs in English, German, and Japanese set the price per photo, with the consent of the subject, at two-hundred *baht*, "all proceeds going to the betterment of village life."

As the delegation trekked toward the headman's house, a gawker in de rigueur safari shirt with roll-up sleeve tabs and a wide-brimmed straw hat shouted at Kay. "Hey! Are you in charge here?" She sounded like an American.

"Why ever would you think that, ma'am?" Kay's voice was sweet as honey, a sure sign she was annoyed. Quinn had heard that tone before, and it did not bode well.

The woman wasn't listening. "How can you let this go on? I have never in my life seen such exploitation, and believe me, I've seen a lot. I've traveled all around the world."

"Really."

"Yes."

"Well, the women don't wear the coils if they don't want to. No one's forcing them. It's an income earner, and they're poor."

"Are you crazy? Don't you know that if they take the rings off, their necks collapse and they suffocate?"

"Nonsense. They pop them on and off all the time. And like I said, they need the money. Ugly truth, but there it is. It's people like you who come here to sneak a look and then pretend to be outraged that keep the thing going. You can stop it, though. Don't come. Or drop a couple hundred bucks at the gift shop. Or here, make a donation to us. Visit our website." She handed the woman a GTEF business card. "We take PayPal," said Quinn, lending help where none was needed.

The woman glanced at the card and stashed it in the zippered money belt under her shirt.

"Can't be too careful," Kay said, nodding at the tourist-only accoutrement.

Watching the woman walk off in a huff, Quinn asked Kay, "Do you really think the rings are okay?"

"What do you think I think? Of course not, it sucks. That's why we're here, Jack, to help with some options if they want them."

When they caught up with their group at Hawhne Shwe's house, refreshments were being served. Taking their places at the low tables, they sat on the floor with their backs cushioned by wedge pillows. Hawhne Shwe toasted the visitors with rice whisky, milky and rancid and served in wooden bowls. Quinn sipped his. Balmer slammed his down, local style.

"Don't want to be rude," he whispered to Quinn while holding out his bowl for a refill.

Kay thanked the villagers for their hospitality with a toast in Thai to good health and prosperity. Just then, the American woman walked by the house, peered in, and whispered to her cohort of well-heeled tourists, pointing to Kay. Kay glared back, and the group moved on.

"Probably upset they didn't get an invite to lunch," Balmer said with a laugh.

After a many-course meal, Hawhne Shwe led the group on a tour of the village and then to the school site. *Khun* Praew walked with him, and Kay and *Khun* Ananda, locked arm in arm, followed. Quinn and Balmer brought up the rear.

"What is that?" Quinn asked as they walked past a small wooden structure with a peaked roof. It appeared to be some sort of chapel. Stained-glass decals covered the two front windows. A cross was affixed to a short steeple. A hand-lettered sign on the front door said, "Saint Pauls."

"Catholic church," explained Balmer. "One of the popes, one of the Innocents, as I recall, sent Italian missionaries to Burma in the seventeen-hundreds. There's still lots of Burmese Catholics. They're animists too, of course. They like holy spirits of all kinds."

Quinn took a look inside the church. He saw rough-hewn pews and a few kneelers in front of an altar. A tabernacle lamp burned red, signifying the presence of God. Paper Stations of the Cross hung along the walls.

"Just like home," he said.

They caught up with the delegation as it was approaching the school site. It was at the edge of the village, removed from the tourist hubbub. Balmer unhooked a tape measure from his belt and began plotting the building's footprint. The group watched as he calculated the degree of slope, figured likely drainage patterns, and checked the position of the sun for good morning exposure and shade in the afternoon.

"No sweat," he said when his calculations were complete. He snapped his tape measure shut.

Hawhne Shwe promised to recruit a village work crew, and *Khun* Praew committed to providing building materials. He handed Kay the rolled-up plans with a finality that indicated the job was now the Foundation's. *Khun* Ananda gave her a list of needed books and supplies, and the two talked on about pedagogy.

As Balmer and Quinn dropped behind, Balmer said, "Let me show you something else."

He led them through the gate of what looked like a livestock fence. A sign screamed, "No Entry!!" and "Extreme Danger!!" Hand-drawn skulls reinforced the warnings.

"Landmines?" asked Quinn.

"Probably not right here, no, but stay on the trail."

Balmer guided them along a well-trodden path that was wide and smooth, more suitable for fast travel than ambling cattle. He pointed to smoke from a campfire visible behind a tree line a few hundred yards away. As they approached, they were intercepted by a squad of guerrillas with assault rifles. Their uniforms were a hodgepodge of shorts and long pants, flip-flops and boots, soft caps and steel helmets, but all wore fatigue shirts with the red screaming-eagle patch of the Karen National Liberation Army. They might have just returned from a cross-border mission. They were mud-spattered and unshaven, and fatigue showed in their eyes.

"You don't want to mess with these dudes," Balmer whispered. "They'll kill you in a minute."

One of the soldiers shouted at them. "What did he say?" Quinn asked.

"Get the fuck out of here, pretty much. They're edgier than usual; sometimes they're almost friendly. There's supposed to be a truce between the military and the Karen, but they're still fighting for independence from Rangoon."

Before, Quinn would have called it Yangon.

Balmer moved his arms slowly down and up and down, trying to calm the situation. The soldiers let them retreat but were in no mood to chat.

Kuhn Praew had noticed them missing and come looking. "Not permitted, not permitted!" he shouted.

He was out of breath when he caught up with them, and his cordiality had disappeared. Schools were all well and good, but allowing glimpses of Karenni rebels operating from Thai territory definitely was not politic. Thailand still did good business with underdeveloped Burma.

"What is wrong with you guys?" Kay said when they were reunited on the safe side of the fence. "Roy, seriously, what are you doing? Don't screw things up here. We need to stick

103

to our knitting, for God's sake."

Balmer muttered, "Sorry, Kay" and showed the signs of mortification an adolescent might display after being caught in some sort of mischief by Sister Superior. He actually looked at his feet for a minute.

Once they got back to the hotel and the deal was sealed with *wais* in the car park, Kay suggested a drink in the bar. Over celebratory clinks of bottles and glass, she told Balmer he was to be paid a generous per diem now, not just actual expenses, and that he could keep his room at the Grande View Hotel until the school was built.

"You're officially on the team now, Roy. And we look forward to working with you for a long time."

Balmer was at a loss for words. But his eyes smiled.

CHAPTER ELEVEN

Performance Review

I N THE MIDDLE OF February, as work was proceeding at Na Soi, Kay approached Quinn at his desk under the stairs.

"It's time for your mid-term evaluation, Jack. And we'd like to know if you're planning on staying with us when your year is up."

Quinn found that encouraging. Until the success of the school construction at Baan Nakha, he hadn't been sure that would be an option.

"Let's do the review at my place," she said. "More private. Tomorrow morning."

While Phen showed absolute discretion, Kay had recruited a few volunteers from the Gymkhana Club who loved to gab while they stuffed and sent new solicitations to mailing lists in the States purchased from like-minded, rural-development NGOs. The new brochures featured photos of the Na Soi project that Balmer sent along with his updates.

Quinn, Kay, and Balmer had agreed that including a few shots of the Paduang women in their neck rings wouldn't hurt. "It is what it is," Balmer said, and Quinn wondered which of the five aggregates of Buddhism covered that.

"Sure," said Quinn. He'd always wanted to see Kay's place. "What time?"

"Any time. Just be on time."

They agreed on nine, and early the next morning Quinn woke with a start. He had just had a nightmare about the

North Koreans kidnapping him, because they needed an American lawyer. Ever since his border visit with Balmer, he'd been having weird dreams.

At eight-thirty, he set out from the Damn Rat, figuring the walk to the high-rise Bunsho Mansions would take no more than fifteen minutes. It couldn't hurt to arrive a little early.

As Quinn walked along the River Ping, he envisioned elephants and mahouts working teak logs down to the sawmills in Chiang Mai, like in the framed nineteenth-century daguerreotype prints at the Gymkhana Club. The ones with Brits in pith helmets supervising the work, hands on their hips.

He crossed the river at the Old Metal Bridge and passed the Khamthiang Flower Market. Watching a procession of saffron-robed monks accepting early-morning offerings of rice and sweets, he bought some marigolds on a whim and gave them to a young novice.

"The monks don't thank you," Kay had explained early on, during one of his cultural-orientation sessions. "Gaining merit is all you get when you make an offering."

But maybe this young monk was new. When he accepted Quinn's offering, the boy said something Quinn didn't understand. He turned left and then right and spun around, looking for assistance.

"He said you have a good heart," the lady who sold him the flowers told him.

Bunsho Mansions dominated the skyline of the diplomatic quarter, northeast of the Old City on grounds the Japanese Army had commandeered for a garrison during World War II. The current occupants were staff from the consulates and Japanese business executives working to keep the co-prosperity sphere humming. Others, like Kay and her husband, were enjoying generous housing stipends from their overseas employers.

When Quinn approached the liveried guard, with his patent-leather belt and highly polished boots, at the security gate, it seemed to confuse him. *Farangs* showing up on foot was unheard of. He was more accustomed to visitors arriving in black chauffeur-driven Toyota Crown Saloons. Once the guard dutifully checked his clipboard, found Quinn's name, and handed him a visitor pass, he let him in the service gate without the salute he gave the cars.

Winding through acres of manicured lawns and almost brutal topiary, the path led past a memorial to Japanese soldiers killed in Burma during the war. A plaque commemorated their deaths from battle wounds, tropical disease, and exhaustion suffered while fighting the Allies. Next to it was a newer marker, this one dedicated to the Aussies, Kiwis, Tommies, and Yanks who had died building Japanese railroads through the jungles while prisoners of war.

The air was still, and the heady scent of late-blooming jacaranda lingered, as did Quinn for a moment, contemplating those on either side of the war. All lost. Same same but different. He mumbled something like a prayer in remembrance of them.

After checking Quinn's name on another list, the elevator attendant pushed the button marked 14. Getting off at the top floor, Quinn proceeded down a hardwood hallway. At the apartment's door, a pair of slip-on sandals and another of Velcroed, rubber-soled walkers were aligned to greet him.

Removal of shoes from a standing position prior to entering a home or temple was a skill Quinn was still developing. Trying to take off a lace-up, he danced around on one foot until he made such a racket banging into the door that Kay opened it before he knocked.

"You need slip-ons," she said. "You're in Asia now."

"Right," Quinn said as Kay grasped his forearm to help stabilize him.

When they reached the living room, Quinn caught a glimpse of Daryl, scooting into one of the upstairs rooms.

"Hi, Daryl!" Quinn shouted.

"Morning, Jack," came the reply from behind the door, reopened a crack. "Working," Daryl said. "Can't talk now."

"*Mai pen rai,*" Quinn said.

What Daryl Kerwin did at the American consulate was a mystery. He maintained such a low profile, folks at the Gymkhana Club speculated that he did some kind of under-cover work dealing with the international drug trade. (Someone told Jack that Daryl had once told someone else he was "on the drug-suppression side.") Everyone knew Thailand was a transshipment point for opium, methamphetamine, and, lately, ketamine from Burma and China. Kay rarely mentioned him.

Now she escorted Quinn to a dining room table big enough to seat twelve at formal affairs. Taking a seat in the middle, she directed him to take the one opposite. He sat down and took in the view.

When Kay offered him coffee or juice or water, Quinn declined.

"No, I'm good," he said. He was anxious to get it over with. He hadn't had a performance evaluation since working for a superior court judge in Seattle in his final year of law school.

Kay opened the personnel jacket in front of her and extracted an evaluation form.

"Read it over," she said, sliding it across the table.

Quinn scanned the document, which mostly rated various performance elements, including communication skills, initiative, accountability, ability to meet deadlines, and teamwork, on a scale of one to five. He had received all fours, "exceeds expectations," except for the three in punctuality.

"You're doing fine, Jack," Kay said as he looked up from the form. "You started off slow, but you're doing fine now.

You turned things around." She seemed in as big a hurry to finish up as Quinn. It was as if they both felt he was too old for this. "Any questions?" she asked. "If not, just sign." She rolled a pen his way.

Quinn signed quickly.

"And date it," Kay said. "Now then. Let's talk about what's next. I know it's early, but do you think you might want to stay on another year? Based on my reports, the board wants you to."

Quinn had met with the governing-board members exactly once, at their monthly meeting when he first arrived. Three men, three women, all American expats. They'd welcomed him before moving on to cluck about expense reports. They could occasionally be bothersome, but they fully supported Kay and gave her free rein. It appeared they had come to see Quinn as adding value.

"What's the rush?"

"If you're definitely not going to re-up, I need to start posting the vacancy on the NGO boards. It's a long lead time filling overseas vacancies."

"To tell you the truth, Kay, I'm not sure."

"Can't commit? Why does that not surprise me, Jack?"

"I think I'd like to stay. Maybe not forever but for another year anyway. I like what we're doing here. I like what I'm doing here."

"Glad to hear it. So what's the hang-up?"

"I told you I have adult children."

"Two."

"Right. Ingrid and Chloe, twenty-eight and twenty-five. Ingrid's a public defender and Chloe teaches elementary school. Both still in Seattle."

"So what's the problem?"

"They think I've gone crazy."

"Really."

"I know. They want to check up on me. They're coming to visit. I need to show them I'm all right."

"When will this be?"

"Soon. Chloe's spring break."

"I can wait a while. In the meantime, if you get more definite one way or the other, let me know." She closed the folder but did not get up.

Quinn leaned back and looked into the living room. It was as expansive as the dining room and as tastefully decorated. The handcrafted sofas were upholstered in nubby green and mauve Thai silk. Glass bookshelves displayed cloisonné pottery and temple rubbings from Bangkok. On the shelves were hardbound classics, which Quinn assumed were Kay's. A large brass American eagle, wings spread, squawked from a top shelf. That would be Daryl's.

A delicately carved bronze Buddha head, about eight inches tall, on a mahogany pedestal drew his attention.

"That's a nice piece," he said, though he didn't know how to evaluate it.

"Sukhothai style, Ceylonese influence. Notice the lotus finial and gentle smile. It's meant to convey compassion and serenity."

Quinn made a mental note to look up "finial" when he got home.

"The Sukhothai Kingdom was established in the thirteenth century," Kay added as they moved to one of the soft couches, "the golden age of Thai architecture and art. The temples in Sukhothai have been beautifully restored. I think the site is better than Angkor."

"How old is it?"

"My Buddha? It's an antique but probably not that old. My guy here in Chiang Mai told me that the piece probably dates from the mid-nineteenth century. There was a huge European market for things Asian back then. All the rage.

Pieces like mine were stolen from temples up and down the country."

"Another missing head."

"There you go. I've thought that too."

"What do you plan to do with it?"

"Take it to one of the temples sometime and give it to a monk. People are doing that now. The monks are glad to get the artifacts—stolen heritage, really—back. And maybe I'll log a few karma miles. Sukhothai is only four hours from here by road. Lovely place. You can ride bikes down the shady paths and view the temples. There are more than a hundred of them. They take your breath away. You should do that sometime."

"You bet. I'd like to do that. The more of the country I see, the better I like it."

Daryl came out of his office just then and peered down into the living room. "You're still here, Quinn?" he asked.

"Just leaving, Daryl. Have a good one!"

CHAPTER TWELVE

Welfare Check

I N EARLY MARCH, a phone call from Ingrid woke Quinn up. "We're coming, Dad, in two weeks," she told him. "I'm sending you the flight information."

"Great," Quinn said. Ingrid had called at six p.m. West Coast time, which was six a.m. in Thailand. Same same but opposite. He tried to shake the cobwebs from his head. "When are you coming, exactly?"

Ingrid paused, apparently referring to her itinerary. "March 15, a Sunday over there. Korean Air to Seoul and then direct to Chiang Mai. Cheapest flight we could find."

From the weekly reports and pictures Balmer was sending, it appeared the work in Na Soi was humming along. It was an easier project than in Baan Nakha, and he had all the help he needed, but sometimes Quinn worried that without Tee's stabilizing influence, Balmer's demons might reappear. He had planned to take another trip north to check things out, but he wouldn't have time for that now.

Fretting about their visit, Quinn began planning a batch of touristic activities to keep his daughters occupied. During slow times at the office, he read about walking tours, museums, and monk chats in his newly acquired *Lonely Planet* guidebook. He started checking restaurant reviews in the *Chiang Mai Mail*.

Two days before his daughters were due in Chiang Mai, Quinn got another early-morning call.

115

"Change of plans, Dad," Ingrid said. "Chloe's not coming after all."

"What happened?"

"Something with the school schedule. Something, something, I don't know."

"Maybe you should cancel too. Wait until you both can come. Summer maybe."

"Too late. Nonrefundable ticket. And I've got my cases moved around. Can't make any more changes. I'll see you in a couple of days."

QUINN WATCHED THE BOEING Triple 7 touch down at Chiang Mai International Airport on a blustery, cloudy morning. Then, waiting in the arrivals hall, he watched the passengers go through baggage search. Ingrid was mid-pack. She picked Quinn out of the crowd and waved, her freshly stamped passport held high.

He presented Ingrid with a sweet-scented jasmine welcome garland from the flower market. They hugged and "Oops," she said, "we crushed it a little."

"It looks beautiful," Quinn replied, straightening it a bit. "And so do you."

"You look good too, Dad. Healthy."

"Never been better," he said and immediately regretted it. "How was the flight?"

"Torture, thanks. If they put terrorists in coach seats for twenty-four hours at Guantanamo, they'd tell you everything you wanted to know."

Ingrid's sharp sense of humor broke the ice.

"Good one," Quinn said, much relieved. "I'll use it."

At the baggage carousel, Ingrid politely waved Quinn off and snatched her jumbo roller bag off the moving belt in one athletic move. Tall and lithe, Ingrid had run track and been a medalist skier in high school.

116

On exiting the terminal, Quinn pointed toward the head of the taxi queue, a hundred yards away. It had started to rain. Ingrid sprinted, the wheels of her bag sending up little rooster tails of spray, and he hurried to keep up.

The cab driver stowed Ingrid's bag and opened the doors for them. He cranked the defroster to hurricane, the windshield cleared, and off they went. "*Bai nai*, where to?" the driver asked, making it sound like one word, "*Bynywherto*," emphasis on the "where."

That was another thing. Ingrid had made it clear she had lodging preferences. She wasn't interested in, as she put it, "Brutalist International style." She wanted a small hotel with local character. "Whatever that is," she had added.

Kay had recommended a place. "*Soi sip-saam*," Quinn told the driver, who nodded. Quinn caught him glancing in the rear-view mirror at Ingrid. "*Luk saa*, my daughter."

"*Suay*, beautiful," the driver observed. Quinn agreed.

Soi thirteen was in the center of Old Town. The driver crawled down a narrow lane barely wide enough for one car until Quinn signaled a stop in front of a nineteenth-century Thai trader's house. The renovated building was painted a brilliant white accented with heavy dark-wood shutters. Slender pillars held up eaves shaped like wings.

"Just what I was looking for," Ingrid said, peering up at the three-story building for a moment before letting herself out of the cab.

"That's classic Lanna architecture."

Quinn had met the owner of the Frangipani Hotel when he'd made Ingrid's reservation. Dressed in a traditional *pha sin* skirt and *sue pat* shirt, she met them at the door and layered Ingrid with a garland of pink roses.

"*Dom rap*, welcome," she said with a *wai* and warm smile.

Ingrid had done her homework. She returned the *wai* in thanks as Quinn carried her bag into the lobby.

"Best room in the house," Quinn assured her on the short elevator ride up.

The elegant suite had furniture upholstered in Thai silk, nicely framed paintings on every wall, teak parquet floors, and soft lighting. Ingrid loved the place. As soon as she found the bedroom, she said, "I think I'll lie down for a bit." The long flight and the time change had her asleep before Quinn could say goodbye. He left her a note on the kitchen fridge, just as he had when she was a kid.

When Quinn returned to the Damn Rat, he pretended to work. Instead, he wasted time on the internet rereading articles about divorce-adjustment disorders in young adults until Ingrid called, two hours later.

"Feeling better now," she said. "I was dead to the world."

"I'll come over."

Ingrid was sitting in the Frangipani's lobby flipping through a new issue of *City Life, Chiang Mai*.

"Anything look interesting?" Quinn asked.

"I have to eat before I can think about anything. I feel like breakfast." It was now late in the day. "I'm all out of whack."

"I know just the place."

Sweetie Pie was a ten-minute walk away. Quinn was disappointed to see that Noi had left for the day; he had hoped to introduce his daughter. They took Quinn's usual spot by the window, and Ingrid began flipping through the multipage menu.

"What do the Thais eat?" she asked.

"For breakfast? *Jok*, rice porridge, and *khanom khrok*, a Thai coconut pancake kind of thing. Sweet."

"I'll have that."

Quinn ordered a burger. "Range-fed Australian beef," he told Ingrid, who leaned vegetarian but didn't care much as long as the animals were treated right.

The table was set, the stage was set, for their initial serious discussion. Quinn took a deep breath.

"You look good, Dad," Ingrid said again after one of Noi's energetic, always smiling servers brought their food. "You have some color; you've lost weight."

"Doing fine."

"So. You're happy here?"

"Sure. I just needed a change. You know that."

Ingrid looked out the window at a pair of tuk-tuks racing down the street. "Looks like you got one, that's for sure."

Quinn didn't bite. "How's Chloe?"

"Stressed, like always."

"She teaches third grade. How hard can that be?"

"Life stresses her. You know that."

"Is she seeing someone?"

"A boyfriend?"

"No. A professional, a therapist of some sort."

"You'd have to ask her."

Chloe had always been a worrier. She took everything too seriously, including the divorce, for which she continued to blame him, though both he and her mother had moved on.

"How's your mom doing?" Liv—the woman he'd married right out of college. They'd met at UW, where she'd been studying architecture and they talked about the Bauhaus and Le Corbusier. Quinn had long ago conceded that Liv was the majority stockholder in Ingrid and Chloe's smarts and Nordic good looks.

"She's dating someone. This time it could be serious."

Quinn desperately wanted to ask who but didn't. He didn't have to.

"Thom Manderly."

Manderly had been a neighbor in Seattle's mainline Laurelhurst neighborhood, where the Quinns had lived before he and Liv sold the house. He taught rhetoric at the university and was a widower. Quinn had thought his wife was nice.

Thom and Liv had gotten to know each other through community theater at the Red Barn Playhouse in Laurelhurst Park. She designed the sets; he often got leading roles. Quinn had seen him badly play a supporting role in Ibsen's *Peer Gynt*. Manderly had pronounced it "Pear." Quinn couldn't stand him.

"Well, good for her. I hope she finds what she's looking for. And you and Chloe are okay with that?"

"Of course." Ingrid paused. "And Dad, we're fine. You don't need to worry about us. We just want to know when you're coming home."

"That's a bit up in the air, I guess."

"Mr. Sanders will give you your job back, right?" William "Sandy" Sanders, who had started working at Safeco at the same time Quinn had, was now head of the legal division.

"Of course. Anytime."

"We still don't understand why you left."

"The thrill was gone."

He knew that sounded glib, even though it wasn't meant to be. He wasn't even sure if Ingrid was referring to the job. He knew that the divorce was mostly his fault. Liv had grown weary of watching Quinn spend the evenings in his recliner, sipping scotch and watching every Mariners game. With the girls grown and gone, she had things she wanted to do—travel, go to Budapest and Tuscany. He mostly wanted to go to bed. Alone. Quinn knew that his passivity had at some point become cruelty. That was not passive. He'd been willing to give up the marriage for everyone's sake. No fault, no recriminations, no squabbling over who got custody of the Belgian Schipperke, Jan.

"I may stay on another year after this one," he told Ingrid.

"Oh, God."

Quinn didn't know if his daughters' disquiet came from genuinely missing him or a fear that he might have passed on some crazy gene that would condemn them to similar irrational acts as they got older. They were still young enough to believe in a preordained universe. Quinn's action had frightened them. He knew that too.

"Look, you're here. We can talk about this more later. Let me show you around a bit. You might like what you see."

CHAPTER THIRTEEN

Sightseeing

QUINN WAS GOING TO show himself around Chiang Mai too. He hadn't made much time for taking in the sights on his own. At first, he wasn't that interested. Now he was too busy.

"Okay. And I want to meet the people you work with."

"Tomorrow night. We're having dinner with Kay, my boss. And our office manager, Phen. You'll like them."

They lingered over their meal. After talking about the trials Ingrid had on her docket (she was doing great), and how her erstwhile boyfriend, in charge of something at Amazon, was doing (not that great), they fell back into the comfort of recalling outings when the girls were little: sailing trips in the San Juans, long ski weekends at Mount Rainier.

Eventually, Ingrid stifled a yawn. "I'm falling asleep again," she said.

"And you'll be wide awake in the middle of the night. It takes a few days for the clock to reset. We'll get a fresh start in the morning."

QUINN ARRIVED AT THE Frangipani promptly at eight and told the taxi driver to keep the motor running. Ingrid was standing out front, reading her own *Lonely Planet* guide.

"Can't we walk?" she asked, seeing the cab.

"I thought we'd start at Doi Suthep, just outside of town. It's a five-thousand-foot mountain with a temple at the top.

Remember? I wrote you it snowed there on Christmas night. It'll give you a chance to stretch your legs and give us a good view of the city if the weather holds."

Late wet-season clouds and showers were possible again that day. But Quinn wasn't thinking only about a clear vista. He figured driving to Doi Suthep and the hike to the temple would take a few hours, spread the day out. He was still worried about awkward downtime in the schedule.

Quinn pointed out the Chiang Mai University campus, the Royal Botanical Gardens, and the zoo as they drove out of the city and began the ascent up the steep, gently winding road. Once on the mountaintop, after leaving cab and driver in the car park and negotiating a phalanx of souvenir vendors, they trod the three hundred and fifty steps to the temple, easily passed by elderly Thai women making their morning offerings.

Ingrid was breathing hard and Quinn was lagging behind when they reached the peak. Ingrid spun prayer wheels and burned incense and received a blessed-string bracelet from one of the monks. The weather was cooperating.

"Spectacular," Ingrid said as she took in the clear view of the mountains and sprawling city below. "This is all otherworldly," she added. Except for a semester abroad in Florence, she hadn't traveled much outside the U.S. and probably had never pictured herself in Asia.

When they got back into town, Ingrid opened her guidebook and pointed out several pictures of thirteenth- and fourteenth-century temples she wanted to see, including Chai Phra Kiat, Si Koet, and Thung Yu, with their glistening red-and-green scalloped-tile roofs and fierce dragon-spirit guardian finials.

They started with Wat Chiang Man. Quinn had seen that one; it was close to her hotel.

"Oldest temple in the city," Ingrid read from her guidebook. "Twelve-ninety-six, built by the great Lanna king Mengrai."

After almost two hours of temple visits, they all began to blend together.

"Seen enough?" Quinn asked.

"Not quite," Ingrid answered. "There are Ramayana murals at Wat Phra Singh," which was all the way across town, the way they had just come.

At Wat Phra Singh, Quinn took a cell-phone picture of Ingrid posing between the two ten-foot-tall, sword-wielding Yaksha demons guarding the front gate. She gladly accepted the offer of a passing sightseer to take a shot of her and Quinn, which she immediately dispatched to friends back home.

"Send me one too," Quinn said.

"Already did. Copied Chloe."

Quinn looked at his watch; it was close to one, and he suggested lunch. "We can go to the club."

"You have a club?"

"The Gymkhana Club." He filled her in as they walked.

"Charming," Ingrid observed without much enthusiasm as they entered the club and walked down the long hallway, lined with daguerreotype prints of club presidents going back to Louis Leonowens. "The sun never sets," she quipped, poking her head into the empty billiards room and the stuffy library.

As they entered the dining room, they were greeted by the Major.

"Haven't see you around here much lately," he said to Jack. "And who might this lovely young lady be?" he asked.

"My daughter, Ingrid, here for a visit."

"Charmed, I'm sure," said the Major. Quinn thought if he'd had a hat, he would have doffed it. "Ingrid," the Major added, "your father is doing God's own work, you know. It must make you proud!"

Ingrid glanced at her father. "It does," she said. The Major led them to a table, even though that wasn't necessary.

The lunch special was Shepherd's Pie. Ingrid had a green salad. Quinn suggested a sweet apple crumble and coffee for dessert. More dawdling time, he figured.

"I'm good," said Ingrid. "I want to see where you live."

"Of course," Quinn said. "It's just a small apartment. Nothing fancy." He didn't tell her that they called the place the Damn Rat.

He opted for a tuk-tuk. They could have walked, but Quinn knew that a tuk-tuk ride was an essential experience in Thailand. Zipping in and out of traffic and tailgating buses may not have been culturally significant, but it was fun. *Sanuk* again.

Quinn chose a raffish-looking driver sporting a long scarf that flew in the wind. He drove wildly, speeding around the traffic circles, and soon Ingrid was laughing as happily as a kid on the teacups at Disneyland.

When the tuk-tuk skidded to a stop in the car park of Quinn's building, he could see Ingrid noted the need for maintenance. The bougainvillea still needed to be trimmed, and a fresh coat of paint still would have helped.

"No pool," said Quinn, as if that were necessary.

Quinn had done his best to tidy the place up a bit. He'd even dusted. Recently, he'd purchased a fifty-five-inch Samsung Ultra-HD flat-screen TV. It made the living room look small, but Quinn had hoped it would show Ingrid he was not living without at least some first-world comforts.

Ingrid cautiously poked around the place. Stepping into the tiny kitchen, she opened a cabinet that revealed Quinn's staples: coffee and sugar, breakfast cereal, canned soup, Dinty Moore beef stew, and ramen. He had a microwave. Ingrid didn't bother to open the fridge but stole a peek into the bedroom. Quinn's clothes were hung neatly in the wardrobe,

126

and she didn't see any socks on the floor. His bed was made.

The inspection didn't take long. When Ingrid seemed satisfied enough, she whisked her hands and said, "Good." And then "I'm fading again. I need another nap."

"Absolutely," said Quinn. "I'll take you back."

"No need, Dad. I can do it." She pulled out a Frangipani Hotel business card from her wallet. "How much should a tuk-tuk be?"

"It's a forty-*baht* ride. They'll ask for eighty, and I usually give fifty. Dinner at six?" he asked.

"Sure. Where are we going?"

"A place called Arun Rai, a locals' spot. Nothing fancy, but Kay says the food is the best Issan fare in town."

A RUN RAI WASN'T FAR from the Frangipani, an open-air shop just across from the Old City Gate. The place was noisy, neon-lit, and basic, with resin chairs and plastic tablecloths; the atmosphere came as much from the green, yellow, and red bottles of fish sauce on the tables as from any attempt at décor. Framed pictures of the king and queen looked down from a place of honor high on the wall.

Kay was there when they arrived, with a garland of flowers, this one of pink orchids.

"So good to meet you, Ingrid," she said, giving her a hug as if they were family. "Your dad has told me so much about you."

"Not all," Quinn said. "Just the good stuff." He didn't usually fall back on such clichés. His nervousness was showing.

When Phen joined them, she *waied* her elders and followed up to Ingrid with a strong fist bump. "Welcome to the Land of Smiles!"

Ingrid replied with a *wai* and a pretty good *Sawadee*.

The menu, no surprise, was in Thai.

"No worries," Kay said. She looked at it for a moment and

then quietly put it down. "I have some favorites, if you'll trust me."

"Absolutely," Ingrid said.

A not-yet-teenage waitress came to their table. Kay introduced her as Nit, the owner's daughter. Nit put down her order pad long enough to smile and *wai*. When she took Kay's order, she didn't need to write it down.

"I ordered Khao Sai, creamy coconut noodle soup. And Gaeng Hung Lay, pork curry. Not too spicy. And the flash-fried marigolds. Heavenly."

"No pad Thai? No sausage?" Quinn asked.

"No."

By the time the second round of Singhas arrived, mid-meal, the conversation had begun to flow as smoothly as the River Ping. Ingrid and Kay were conversing like old friends who hadn't seen each other in ages.

Ingrid talked mostly with Phen, though. They had connected immediately, and in response to one of Ingrid's questions, Phen told her she would show her the tailor shop where she had her business suits made.

"I'm thinking of going to law school," Phen said later in the conversation.

"We need to talk," Quinn said.

"We're hiring," Ingrid said.

Quinn was beginning to feel relaxation beyond the effects of the beer. Maybe this was all going to work out, he thought. Maybe Ingrid was relieved to see that he hadn't gone full Kurtz and disappeared up the river. Maybe she felt that things with them would be all right.

When the meal was over, Kay grabbed the check.

"Business expense," she said, but she didn't wait for a receipt. And then, to Ingrid, "Want to walk a bit? You should see the Night Bazaar."

"And then we can stop by the U.N. Irish Pub for a nightcap," Quinn said. "NGO workers and expats."

"Zoe in Yellow, right next door, is better," Phen told them. "Younger crowd."

The Night Bazaar consisted of stalls spanning both sides of Chang Khlan Road, in the most touristy part of town. The anonymous high-rise hotels, the kind Ingrid hated, loomed over McDonalds, Sizzler, Kentucky Fried, and Starbucks outlets. "We call it Saint Arbucks," Kay said, referring to the coffee chain. "The Crusades are not yet over."

The three-block-long night market pedaled the usual knockoff Polo, Chanel, and Rolex merchandise tourists hankered for. Xboxes, DVDs, and CDs competed for space with switchblades, nunchucks, Red Bull T-shirts, and the four-dollar collared shirts and extra-large cargo pants bought in bulk by expats on a budget. And luggage.

"About the only thing real on this street is the *baht* in your purse," Phen confided. "Save your money."

But Ingrid was on a mission for souvenirs, and Kay directed her to a stall selling colorfully embroidered Lahu shoulder bags.

"Good, easy to pack," Ingrid said.

As she methodically selected several, one by one, from a large pile, she was approached by a tribal woman with a silver-bead-and-coin-encrusted headdress.

"She's Akha," Quinn whispered. "We built the school for them."

The woman was selling whirligigs that made a sound like buzzing cicadas. In one arm, she cradled a swaddled infant, sleeping soundly through the racket. Ingrid studied the baby and said to the mother, "*Suay,*" the word she had heard the day before that meant "beautiful."

The Akha woman offered the infant to Ingrid to hold, which she did, swaying it back and forth lightly a few times before trying to hand it back. The woman resisted, as if she wanted Ingrid to keep the baby. Ingrid gently shook her head, gave the child back, and bought all the trinkets the woman had.

The next morning, Quinn met Ingrid at the hotel as usual. They were planning on visiting an elephant refuge that day, with Noi's tour-guide friend Samorn. And maybe the next day a celadon kiln or the famous hand-painted-parasol factory the guidebooks recommended. Ingrid was waiting on a couch in the lobby, and before she noticed him, Quinn heard her say into her phone, "He's fine."

CHAPTER FOURTEEN

The Crossroads

B Y LATE APRIL, THE Na Soi school was finished, right on time. Quinn and Kay had already lined up another project, this one in Mae La, a Karen refugee camp in the border province of Tak. Fighting was intensifying in Burma, and the Thai government was trying to do something to help. The proposed school was like the one in Na Soi, simple, off-the-shelf plans, with the Thai Refugee Commission paying for building materials and supplies.

"Roy needs a break," Kay said. "He's been working for months, and Tak is no garden spot."

"Been thinking the same thing," said Quinn, although he thought working to exhaustion might be when Balmer felt best. "Give him a few weeks off before we start? With pay?"

"Yes and yes."

"I'll call him tomorrow morning."

THE CELL-PHONE SIGNAL in Fang was strong. It sounded like Balmer was right next door. "Hi, Jack. Have a date set for Tak?"

"Yes, but how about taking a few weeks off before you start? Paid?"

"You're reading my mind. I've been itching to take a good long bike ride along the Mekong. All the way to Nong Khai. Let the calluses soften."

"Nong Khai?"

"A laid-back little town just across the Mekong from

Vientiane. It's one of the best rides in Asia—mountains, jungles, fast rivers, no traffic. All the things you'd like. Hey, you should come along."

"I don't ride. Never have," said Quinn. Not counting the expensive road bike he had bought for exercise and used a few times before hanging it on a rack in his garage.

"No matter. You can ride with me."

"On the same bike?"

"Sure. Why not?"

"I don't think that's a good idea."

"Too *Easy Rider*?"

"Something like that."

"Well, here's an idea. I have an Aussie buddy who picked up an old Russian army motorcycle in Laos. Olive drab with a red star on the sidecar. Very cool. You can ride in that."

"He's going?"

"He doesn't know it yet, but he never passes up a chance for a good ride. Maybe I'll invite Tee too. He loves riding the Superhawk. We can rent him one of those new Yamahas."

"He's back in school full time."

"He told me that was his plan. I just wasn't sure when. Well, no matter. You come."

Quinn thought for a minute.

"Okay, sure. Let me check with Kay to see if I can get the time off."

He disconnected and called up to Kay in her office.

"Can I have a few days off too? Roy wants me to join him on a motorcycle ride."

She didn't answer his question. "Jack, could you come on up for a minute?"

Once he climbed the stairs and saw Kay at her desk, he noticed her eyes were red. He was so surprised, he sat down in the chair across from her without being asked. He had never seen her cry.

"What's up, Kay? Bad news? Are we broke?"

"Nothing like that. Daryl told me this morning he's cutting his tour short. He's asking to be reassigned. He didn't talk to me about it. Unilateral decision."

"I thought he liked it here."

"He says he's bored. Not enough action. And promotions come more quickly somewhere else. He thinks he wants Ukraine."

"So when does all this happen? And what do we do without you? I'm not sure GTEF can stay afloat." He was sure it would not.

"Well, that's the other part of the story, I guess. I'm not going with him."

"You're sure about this, Kay? You two have been together a long time. Right?"

"Years."

"So maybe you should slow down. Step back a bit, think about it."

"It's too late for that. This has been brewing for a long time."

Kay didn't seem averse to talking, so Quinn stayed where he was.

"Forgive me, Kay, but how did you two ever get together in the first place? You seem like such different people. Now, anyway."

"You're right. We weren't always. We met in Texas—he was studying international relations at Austin, and I was an English major."

"I thought you were from North Carolina?"

"I was. Chapel Hill."

"UNC. That's a good school. Why didn't you go there?"

"I wanted to get out of town. Stifling. Anyway, Daryl was an army brat from El Paso. He wanted to join the State Department. I wanted to travel. So after graduation, we went to D.C. State wasn't interested, but he got picked up by the foreign office of the Drug Enforcement Agency. I got my masters in English at George Mason University. Tried teaching Faulkner at a junior college. That didn't work out well, so I got my certificate in teaching English as a Second Language. Daryl was in line for an assignment overseas, and I figured I could teach anywhere."

"So what's happened between you and Daryl?"

"We drifted apart, that's all—gradually, over time. It happens. He got more conservative, and I've stayed as liberal as I always was. That's the way I see it anyway. He believed that old saw about if you're not liberal when you're young, you have no heart; and if you're not conservative when you're old, you've got no brain. I always thought I had a better brain than he did."

Quinn tended to agree.

"And it didn't help that Daryl knew I thought that," Kay said.

"I guess not. Never had kids?" Quinn asked.

"Nope."

"So how soon is this all happening?"

"It mostly depends on when Daryl gets his new assignment. Could be a few weeks, could be a few months."

"You know what, Kay? You should take some time off too. Get away from all this for a while. Things are under control here right now. Phen can run things."

"I'll think about it," Kay said. "Thanks for asking." She stood up and patted him on the arm.

Quinn waited until Kay went out for lunch at Sweetie Pie, probably to talk to Noi, and then called Balmer back.

"So Kay's okay with you coming on the ride?"

"No problem. She may take some time off too. Daryl's giving her some shit."

"He seemed like a very uptight guy the time I met him."

"He is. So when do we ride?"

"A fortnight."

Quinn wasn't sure if that was an affectation or if Balmer was picking up on expat lingo. Probably the latter, he figured.

TWO WEEKS LATER, QUINN tuk-tukked to the long-haul Arcade bus terminal and boarded a nonstop bus to Chiang Rai, Chiang Mai's little sister, a hundred and eighty-five kilometers north. Kay stayed in Chiang Mai, nursing the foundation and herself.

Bus rides were now a regular part of Quinn's life. He had the drill down: the first-class seat, the earplugs, one Ambien from a legit pharmacy that didn't sell fakes from India. He was dead to the world in thirty minutes and awakened four hours later by the gentle touch of the smiling bus stewardess.

"Chiang Rai," she announced in a soft tone that made alarm clocks seem intentionally annoying.

Balmer's instructions were specific. They were to meet up with his biker pal at the Crossroads Saloon, across the street from the bus depot.

"Guy's name is Ridley," Balmer had told Quinn. "He's an Aussie. Likes to be called Ryder."

Quinn grabbed his small duffel from the overhead rack, lurched off the bus, and stumbled over to the Crossroads. Parked in front of the Western-style saloon were carefully backed-in Harleys, big-engine Hondas and Yamahas, BMWs, and the odd Moto Guzzi. Ridley was easy to spot. He was sitting alone on the broad front porch, black boots on the railing and his chair tilted back, obviously waiting for someone. He wore a black bandana, low, like a neck scarf.

"Ridley?" Quinn asked as he approached.

"Ryder," he corrected. He was not at all what Quinn had expected. Describing someone as an Aussie biker brought to mind a certain image: big, muscled arms with lots of tattoos, a beard and scowling looks. Ryder's tattoos looked too big on his skinny arms, and his leather vest with the "Chiang Rai Outlaws" patch wasn't fooling anyone. A pointed black goatee gave him a slightly devilish look.

"You must be Roy's mate," he said. "Still waiting for him to arrive."

Which didn't take long. Balmer rolled up on the Superhawk before Quinn had finished his cup of clear-the-cobwebs coffee. He clomped onto the porch slapping road dust from his jeans. Once he gave Ryder a bro hug and then one to Quinn, he sat down hard on a wooden chair and ordered a beer.

"Long time, mate," Ryder said to Balmer. "Where've you been? We've missed you at the rallies."

"Upcountry," Balmer said. "Doing some work."

Which could mean anything in that part of the world, but Ryder didn't inquire. "Brilliant" was all he said.

Ryder already had a beer in front of him. As soon as Quinn and Balmer got theirs, the biker buddies began recalling previous rides in northern Thailand, especially the thousand-kilometer trek down the southern peninsula all the way to Malaysia.

"Phuket. Better beaches than Bondi," Ryder said.

Balmer nodded in agreement and then asked, "Remember the ride to Siem Reap? That place still gives me the creeps."

"They can't all be winners."

"So where are we headed?" Quinn asked after what he thought had been adequate time for catching up.

Balmer took a plastic road map from his vest, pushed aside their drinks, and spread it out on the low wooden table.

"We're doing the Uttaradit Loop," he said, tracing it with his finger. "East along the Mekong on Highway 211. Lunch in Nan town tomorrow—really good Indian place there. Then we'll head up into the mountains."

"Book us at the Mountain Lodge?" Ryder asked.

"Where else?" said Balmer. "There's hot springs there," he told Quinn.

"Super wildlife viewing at the resort," Ryder added. "Here's the brochure," he said, pronouncing it *brasure*, European style. Quinn saw the Mountain Lodge boasted of the barking deer, macaques, masked civets, monitor lizards, and shrews in the area. "Great birding too, and we might see a tiger."

"There are no tigers," Balmer said.

"Indochinese tiger, *Panthera tigris corbetti*. But yes, very rare," Ryder conceded.

Balmer shook his head and continued with the briefing. "We'll take the trip slow and easy. Grand-touring style. No racing."

"Agreed. Ivan isn't into competitions anymore."

"Your motorcycle?" Quinn asked. "When can I see it?"

"It's parked out back."

The Ural motorcycle was as Quinn had imagined it: Squatting on spindly, wire-spoke wheels, it was big, heavy, and clumsy looking.

"See how you fit in the sidey," said Ryder.

Quinn wriggled into the sidecar and found ample room for his legs, but he had to sit straight up.

"How's she ride?" he asked.

"A bit rough. Dampers are pretty much shot. You'll need a cushion."

"Where do I get a cushion here?"

"Chemists across the street. They have medical supplies. Get a wheelchair pad or something."

Pushing himself up and requiring minimal assistance from Ryder and Balmer, Quinn extricated himself from the sidecar.

"Could be worse," he said.

They returned to their chairs on the front porch, where

Ryder and Balmer fell into an arcane discussion about motor-cycle repair. When they got into the knuckle-busting task of rebuilding cylinder heads, Quinn interrupted.

"Where are we sleeping tonight?"

"Cadillac Hotel, next to the drugstore," Balmer said. "Get a room in the back if you can. It can get noisy here around midnight. We'll meet tomorrow at nine a.m. No need to leave at the crack of dawn. We're on vacation."

In the brightly lit drug store, Quinn couldn't find any therapeutic pads, but he did locate neck pillows and bought two, figuring he could make a suitable donut from the pair. Purchase made, he walked next door to the Cadillac Hotel. A mock-up of a 1950s De Ville grill with working headlights served as the marquee. In the lobby, old car seats were repur-posed as couches.

He requested a room in the back as suggested, and he got one, but it didn't help much. At exactly twelve o'clock, a herd of bikes were fired up, revved to red line, and then sped up and down the street for an hour. Quinn thought he could feel the windows shake. He put in his earplugs to shut out the cacophony, but the vibration lingered.

The next morning, he found Balmer tinkering with the Superhawk in front of the Crossroads. Ryder was already there too.

"Front brake seemed a little spongy yesterday," Balmer explained.

He removed a tool pouch from one of the saddlebags, put on a pair of knee pads, and knelt to make an adjustment to the disk. It looked like he had done this before. Attempting to tighten the brake cable with a crescent wrench, he found it wouldn't budge.

"I'm not finding a whole lot of Zen in this," he muttered.

"Try a bigger spanner," Ryder suggested.

Balmer glared at him but grabbed a wrench with a longer

handle. Once he prized the reluctant connector loose and adjusted the cable tension, he stood up, knees bent, flexed the brake lever several times, then rolled the bike forward to test the repair.

"Perfect," he said.

After stowing his tools, Balmer mounted his bike and hit the starter button. Which was the cue for Ryder, all one hundred and thirty-five pounds of him, to stand on the Ural's kick starter and drive it down with every ounce of strength he had in his body. Fortunately, the bike fired up on the second try. It didn't look as if he had a third attempt in him.

"Saddle up," he told Quinn over the Ural's slow, rough idle. "Or should I say take your seat?"

Quinn stowed his bag in the boot of the Ural's sidecar and extracted the neck pillows.

"What in bloody hell are those?" Ryder asked.

"Butt savers," Quinn said. He shimmied into the sidecar, wriggled around a bit on the pillows, and gave Ryder a thumbs up. He thought he could see an eye roll behind Ryder's goggles.

Balmer handed Quinn a helmet. "Can't be too safe," he told him.

CHAPTER FIFTEEN

The Ride

BALMER CLUNKED THE SUPERHAWK into gear, and Ryder, maybe just to show off a bit, shifted the Ural into reverse to get in line behind him. Now Balmer gave a thumbs up, smiled and nodded, and led the way down Chiang Rai's main drag toward the highway. "The 211," Balmer called it, as if they were in L.A.

The nascent urban sprawl of fast-growing Chiang Rai quickly disappeared, and soon they reached open country, with soft-shouldered foothills all around them and the sharp peaks of the Mae Salong Range in the distance.

As they left Chiang Rai behind, Quinn began for the first time to experience the joys of motorcycle riding. The morning was still cool, the air smoke free, the sun warm on his face. Daubs of color flew past: the pale umber of drying tobacco leaves, the brilliant orange of heavily laden citrus trees, the deep vermillion of mounds of chili peppers by the side of the road.

And the smells: village cook fires and the sweet scent of newly tilled soil intermixed with the funk of ambling livestock. All overlaid with heady diesel fumes from passing trucks and buses and the hot-oil smell of the bike engines.

The spell was broken when Balmer pulled over for a smoke.

"How're the brakes?" Ryder asked as the Ural pulled up beside him.

"A bit grabby. May have over-tightened the caliper. But I

think they'll be okay."

"And how are you doing, mate?" Ryder asked Quinn. The drone of the Ural's engine had made communication en route almost impossible.

"Couldn't be better!" Quinn enthused.

Ryder watched him peel the carcass of a large fruit fly off his cheek.

"Sometimes you're the bug, sometimes you're the windscreen."

"Sometimes you're the hammer, sometimes you're the nail."

"Sometimes you eat the bear, sometimes the bear eats you."

"Yes," said Quinn.

Smoke break over, Balmer field-stripped his cigarette and put the filter in his chest pocket for later disposal, just as he had been instructed by his drill sergeants.

"The army was always concerned about litter," he said when he noticed Quinn observing the ritual.

The Ural's big twin-cylinder engine produced more noise than power, and on the long uphill grades, the light Superhawk easily pulled away. It was the same on the serpentine stretches, where Balmer leaned his bike, one leg out, roadracer style, and disappeared around the bends, leaving the Ural in his wake.

The bikes played cat-and-mouse for two hours before reaching the ancient town of Nan. For centuries, various Thai, Lao, and Burmese kingdoms had battled for sovereignty over the kingdom of Nan, with the Thai Lanna finally taking control in the eighteenth century. Thousand-elephant temples, Hindu-Khmer prayer towers dedicated to Shiva and Vishnu, and Thai lotus-blossom *chedis* had all left their marks on the landscape.

They stopped in front of a Buddha statue fronting a crumbling fourteenth-century city wall. Balmer *waied* deeply and then turned to Quinn.

"Subduing Mara posture," he said of the statue's pose. "See how the right hand is fingers up toward heaven, for enlightenment? And the left is pointed down toward the ground, showing rejection of human desire." Quinn *waied* too.

In the middle of town, Balmer took a left turn and picked his way down a narrow *soi* until they reached the Dheevaraj restaurant.

"The DeeVee, locals call it," Balmer announced. "Best Punjabi food in northern Thailand. I recommend the buffet."

They paid their two-hundred-*baht* gate fee to an imposing Sikh behind the counter. The place was redolent with the aroma of roasting lamb. At the buffet table, *roti* flatbread and vegetable *kadai masala* competed for space with kebabs, rich and mild Massaman curry, tandoori chicken, and a giant pot of *dal* soup. Following Balmer's lead, Quinn and Ryder forewent the featured Jaipur lager and drank traditional Indian *lassi*, a blend of yogurt, water, and spices; they ordered theirs with mango and papaya.

"Need to stay sharp," Balmer said. He took the free refill.

After lunch, they picked up the highway and backtracked a few kilometers to exit on a secondary road, unmarked except for a dusty hand-painted sign with an arrow indicating the way to Mountain Lodge.

The road climbed steeply toward the two-thousand-meter peak of Doi Phu Kha, where they pulled over at a traffic turnout amid several tourist vans. Small groups of mostly *farang* birders were scanning the treetops with Zeiss and Nikon binoculars. One, his billed cap turned backward, was squinting into a scope on a tripod.

"There!" Ryder called out. "Chestnut-crowned laughing thrush, three o'clock, twenty feet up."

"See it!" some said, turning in unison, while others kept looking.

After a few kilometers of rough road, they reached the

lodge, snugged into a small cleft in the mountainside. When they pulled up to the reception office, a smiling young man wearing a polo shirt with the establishment's mountains-in-the-mist logo came out to greet them.

"Dehk," he introduced himself after giving them a group *wai*. His nametag identified him as "Owner Manager."

Balmer looked over at the cluster of simple A-frame cabins.

"Can one of your units handle us all?" he asked.

"They all have two single beds and a sofa sleeper," Dehk said. "Bunks too."

"Do you have an end unit?" Ryder inquired.

"Sorry, we're heavily booked."

"What does it matter?" Balmer asked.

"You need silence to hear the night song."

As they walked over to inspect the cabin, a Siamese cat bounded from the office. "Wildlife!" shouted Quinn, snapping a photo to be captioned "Tiger on the loose" to send to Ingrid and Chloe.

"Close to the hot springs," Dehk said as he unlocked the front door. "We have *yukatas*," he added, gesturing toward the blue-and-white cotton Japanese robes on hooks by the door to wear to the hot springs. "Dinner is at six."

"I'll take a bunk," said Ryder. "Close to the windows."

Dehk tested the mini fridge for coolness and then held out the room key, on an elephant-head wooden paddle that would float and be hard to lose. Ryder hooked it onto a carabiner attached to his belt. As he padded around the room, the key rubbing against the wood made a whispering sound.

Dehk excused himself from the room with a slight bow. "Nearby are trails, limestone caves, and waterfalls too."

"Got any beer, Dehk?" Ryder asked as he was leaving.

"Plenty. Just got a delivery of Tsingtao."

"Chinese beer," Balmer scowled. "The Chinese will rule the world one day, but they can't brew a decent pilsner."

"I have Singha," Dehk said. "Better."

"Ching ching," Ryder affirmed.

Ryder followed Dehk to the small store off the reception office, where he grabbed two six-packs from the cooler and threw in a jumbo bag of shrimp chips. Dehk double-bagged the purchases in plastic and tossed in a few napkins.

Back at the room, Ryder handed out beers before stowing the remainder in the humming fridge, now set on high. All the cabins had deck chairs for taking in the mountain views, and they repaired to theirs. Balmer went back in for the chips.

The late-afternoon sky was clear, but a steady breeze blew down from the summit of Doi Phu Kha and the temperature was dropping quickly. No one had bothered to bring a warm jacket.

"The robes," Balmer suggested.

He went inside to grab them and a few more beers. Once bundled up on the deck, they could have been aging Japanese men at an ancient Kyoto *onsen*. And then Balmer suggested a dip.

"It's totally relaxing," he told Quinn, who was feeling pretty relaxed already.

At the steaming hot springs, Balmer stripped to his skivvies and plunked himself into the pungent green sulfur pool.

"Water's fine," he announced. Quinn joined him. Ryder rolled up his pants and sat on the edge, dangling his legs. The only sound was that of the birds in the grove of sweet pink-flowering apple trees that surrounded them.

"Black-eared shrikes," Ryder offered. "Hear how they're saying, 'Where're you going, dutta dut dutdut, dutta dut duduut?' Bird mnemonics." Quinn thought he could hear it.

After the better part of an hour, when Quinn and Balmer's chests were pink and Ryder's feet were puckered, they padded, shoes and boots untied, back to the lodge. A small group of birders, still in their subdued brown-and-green birding shirts, were gathering in front of the restaurant, The Roost, waiting for the dinner sitting to begin.

"Let me check the specials," Balmer said, scanning the posted bill of fare. "Hey, *stu kratai* is on."

"What's that?" Quinn asked.

"Rabbit stew."

They went back to the cabin long enough to change out of their wet clothes and grab the remaining beers.

"No corkage," Balmer assured them.

Dehk, now serving as waiter, brought them a bucket of ice. Balmer went for the rabbit stew, and Quinn for the *pho* that was getting popular outside Vietnam. Ryder selected the mixed tofu.

"Sometimes I eat meat," he said, as if justification were needed.

Slurping his soup, Quinn asked Balmer, "Where do we go tomorrow?"

"Town called Phitsanulok. Two hundred klicks."

As they finished their meal, Quinn noticed that Balmer was fidgeting. Drumming his fingers on the table and looking around the room, he seemed distracted. Leaving a half-drunk beer on the table but finishing his rabbit stew, he said he was going to turn in early. "Beat" was all he said.

Which left Quinn and Ryder alone to talk. There wasn't much to say. Quinn didn't know anything about the Sturgis Motorcycle Rally, and Ryder didn't care about football, even the Australian kind. Soon they followed Balmer back to the cabin.

Balmer was breathing deeply and regularly, almost as if he was meditating. His pillow was on the floor. Was he mumbling, Quinn wondered, or was it a mantra?

CHAPTER SIXTEEN

Bend in the Road

AT SIX THE NEXT morning, Balmer roused Quinn and Ryder with fake toots of "Reveille."

"Drop your cocks and put on your socks, ladies!" he bellowed, drill-sergeant style. And just like in the army, basic trainees Quinn and Ryder grumbled and wiped sleep from their eyes before planting their feet on the floor. "Be ready to ride in thirty!" Balmer commanded.

He was sitting on his bike drinking a coffee when Quinn and Ryder hustled out of the lodge a half-hour later. Quinn leaned against the sidecar and did a few calf stretches before climbing in. Ryder saddled up and pulled out the choke to fire up the engine.

The day started out favorably. The Ural fired up on the first try. Quinn scooched into the sidecar, and Balmer hit the electric start on the Superhawk. He flexed the brake levers a few times and pronounced them fine.

"Use low gears," he advised Ryder. They descended the mountain slowly, pulling over every ten minutes or so to let the brakes cool. Balmer was being overly cautious, it seemed to Quinn.

They made good time, covering seventy kilometers in less than an hour. Quinn saw the wide, swift-moving river off to the left and the catchment area created by the Queen Sirikit hydroelectric dam up ahead. The lake was as sapphire blue as Lake Tahoe. The distant, jutting peaks could have been the Sierra if the ridges were just a bit edgier, and the dam could have been the Hoover. Where, Quinn wondered, was he exactly?

As the highway steeply sloped down toward the dam, Ryder down-shifted, but Balmer inexplicably sped up. He was going faster and faster. Quinn looked for a brake light but didn't see one. What he did see was Balmer madly flexing the brake levers, with no effect.

The roadway curved sharply where it crossed the top of the dam. Balmer's bike began wobbling from side to side as he desperately tried to regain control. He couldn't do it. The Superhawk flew off the road at high speed, launched into a high parabola, and, after what seemed an impossibly long time, crashed on the rocks of the spillway, four hundred feet below.

Ryder pulled over where the Superhawk had left the road. A cross-country bus stopped near them, and its passengers got off to gape over the edge while the driver radioed for help. Quinn and Ryder simply stood in shocked silence. Except for random utterances. "Too much speed." "Brakes." "This can't be happening." "He didn't make it."

It wasn't long before they heard sirens wailing, and a rescue crew, a fire truck, and an ambulance, red lights flashing, pulled in next to them. One of the crew looked down over the spillway and shook his head. Quinn, feeling like he was sleepwalking, joined him. Balmer's body was twenty feet away from the crumpled bike. The sirens stopped. The rescue mission had become a recovery.

A few minutes later, a police unit showed up, and a sergeant approached. The parked Ural and the two stunned riders were the connection to the wreck he was looking for. The officer took one look at Ryder and then turned his attention to Quinn. He *waied*, first toward the body of Balmer, at the bottom of the dam, and then to Quinn. "*Sow*, sad," he said to them and then *"Khathot,* sorry.*"*

The sergeant handed Quinn a business card with the address of the provincial police station in Uttaradit.

"Tomorrow," he said, pronouncing it *tummolo,* Thai style, giving it a light, evanescent sound.

The fire crew slowly began lowering a metal litter down the cliff. Quinn couldn't bear to see Balmer bumping up the cliff in a body bag in a wire basket. It seemed the final, undeserved insult.

He and Ryder got back on the Ural and motored slowly the few miles to Uttaradit. They found a business hotel off the highway that offered free wi-fi and a cocktail lounge. Quinn knew he was in need of both.

They went straight to the bar, a dark space off the lobby. It featured karaoke at night but had no customers so early in the day. Quinn and Ryder's conversation consisted of aphorisms about the fragility of life, a good way to go, doing what one loved, no suffering, until Quinn said, "I think he knew it might be coming, at least sooner rather than later."

"How do you reckon?"

"Whenever we talked about what's next, he took the short view. I never heard him talk about what he'd be doing five years from now. I think he tried to live in the present."

"Yeah, he didn't have a bucket list," said Ryder. "He looked down on people who do. Just live life is what he thought."

"Maybe that came from studying Buddhism. I don't know that it brought him…well, peace of mind," Quinn reflected, thinking now perhaps nothing could have done that, "but it gave him a way to look at life. A good way."

"He didn't seemed too worried about dying, that's for sure. It was like he always had his bag packed. Ready to go at any time."

When the front-desk clerk came over, they ordered beers from him. Quinn asked for three, one for Balmer.

"Did you know him long?" Quinn asked.

"A few years. It was mostly the bikes."

Then silence, until Ryder said after quickly draining his beer, "Look, sorry, but I'm going to have to head back to Chiang Rai. There's nothing I can do here. You were his mate; can you handle the arrangements?"

Quinn understood. Ryder hadn't signed on for this. He had been looking for another road trip, hoping to spot a tiger or at least a rare Oriental White Eye Finch. That was it.

Ryder scribbled his email address on a bar napkin. "Let me know if there are any services," he said, and then he was gone.

Quinn drank his beer slowly, and then started in on the one he had ordered for Balmer. It was then that he began to feel Balmer's presence. Quinn thought he could see him, sitting in a chair in some kind of far-off waiting room or reception hall. He was smiling. His maroon shirt was pressed and his shoes were gleaming.

"Where are you, Roy?"

"I'm in the Sipda, Jack. Kind of like a Tibetan Limbo. I'm waiting here, being processed for my next gig."

"How is it up there?"

"Nice. Peaceful."

"Did you feel any pain?"

"None at all. I don't even remember it."

"Glad to hear it. Any idea where you're going next?"

"Looks like a better assignment this time around, maybe. Maybe another planet where things are more squared away. I'm hopeful."

"Glad to hear it, Roy. You've earned it."

"Thanks, man. And hey, Jack, this is all easy. No big deal. You don't have to worry."

"Thanks, Roy. That's good to know."

"No problem. Call me anytime. I'll always answer."

CHAPTER SEVENTEEN

Final Arrangements

A FTER A SLEEPLESS NIGHT, Quinn asked at the hotel's reception desk for directions to the police station. A young man came from behind the counter and led Quinn outside.

"*Nit noi*," he said, pointing in the direction of the Nan River. *Nit noi*. Another Thai phrase that could indicate many things, including small in stature, a little bit of something, or a short distance or amount of time.

Quinn walked a few blocks down the road and easily found the precinct house, made a little bit more welcoming by its koi pond out front. When he showed the desk sergeant the card he'd been given the day before, he was directed with a nod to a sign with a string of Thai characters and the words "Medical Examiner" in English. An arrow pointed into the basement.

At the bottom of the stairs, Quinn opened a thick glass door and felt the temperature drop sharply. A young woman sitting at a reception desk, wearing a sweater over her white coat, smiled just enough to put him at ease.

"*Khun* Roy Balmer?" she asked.

"Yes."

She went to a shelf behind her and took a stapled-shut paper bag from among several sitting there.

"Final effects," she said, handing the parcel over. "Please check them."

Quinn opened the bag and placed its contents on the counter. There wasn't much there: keys on a ring, a plastic lighter, the pliers, a wallet with a Thai driver's license, credit and debit cards, and about a hundred dollars in *baht*. In one of the slots was a worn, folded-over copy of a prayer by Thomas Merton.

> *"My Lord God,*
> *I have no idea where I am going.*
> *I do not see the road ahead of me.*
> *I cannot know for certain where it will end....*
> *I know you will lead me by the right road,*
> *Though I may know nothing about it.*
> *Therefore will I trust you always,*
> *Though I may seem to be lost and*
>   *in the shadow of death.*
> *I will not fear, for you are ever with me,*
> *And you will never leave me to face my perils alone."*

At the bottom of the paper bag, in a smaller plastic one, was the Buddha amulet on a heavy gold chain that Balmer always wore.

"For protection and grounding," he had explained to Quinn when asked about it. "I need both."

Quinn knew that Balmer had been raised a Christian, and the Merton prayer seemed to confirm it. Was he hedging his bets with the Buddhist talisman? But then, he had read enough to find elements he liked in the various belief systems he had encountered along the way.

"You ditch the lace and incense and chants, and you'll find all religions are pretty much going in the same direction," Balmer had said. "Pick and choose from column A and column B, and you'll be fine." He seemed to have faith but no orthodoxy. Quinn thanked him for the dharma.

A fortyish man with just-graying hair, also in a white coat, came out from the back.

"I'm Doctor Arthrit," he said, shaking Quinn's hand, "the medical examiner. These things are all we were able to save," he told Quinn. "It was a bad crash."

"That's fine, Doctor." Quinn was already feeling weighed down by the few things Balmer had carried. "That's fine."

"Are you next of kin?"

"No. A friend. He has no family that I know of."

"You'll take responsibility then?"

"For what?"

"Disposition of the remains."

"Yes."

"Do you know what religion he was?"

"Hard to say. Probably Buddhist." Quinn thought he'd keep things simple.

"Wat Tha Thanon is across the street. They do our cremations. If you want, we can make those arrangements and forward the remains on to you."

"I think that would be best," Quinn said. He pulled out his own wallet.

"You don't need to worry about that now," said Doctor Arthrit. "We'll send you a statement later." He pushed a sheaf of papers, all in Thai, across the counter and showed Quinn where to sign. "No need to view the body," he said. "Unless you want to."

"I don't."

Quinn climbed the stairs to the first floor and was aware of people watching him as he crossed the lobby. He assumed they thought he had just been released from lockup and were curious what kind of shenanigans another *farang* had gotten himself into. The desk sergeant said something in Thai to the onlookers, who responded to Quinn with *wais*.

At Wat Tha Thanon, Quinn sat on a bench under a pipal

tree in the courtyard. White smoke was coming from the tall chimney of the crematorium behind the temple. It was time to let Kay know.

She answered on the first ring. "What's up, Jack? I thought you'd be out of range."

Quinn pictured Kay in her office, flipping through papers as she spoke and hoping the conversation would be brief because she had work to do. But when Quinn said, "Bad news," he saw her shifting her focus and staring into the near distance.

"What is it?" she asked.

"It's Roy. There was an accident."

"Yes?"

"He didn't make it, Kay."

A momentary silence, and then, "What happened?"

"We think the brakes on his motorcycle failed. He might have been going too fast, and he went off the road." Quinn didn't see any need for further details and wasn't sure he was ready to give them anyway.

"What can I do?"

"Nothing right now. Roy's being cremated here in Uttaradit. I'll take a bus to Fang to check at his house. Maybe he left a will."

The only option was a local bus, which stopped whenever and wherever a passenger flagged it down or rang the buzzer to get off. It took five hours to cover the two hundred kilometers to Fang.

Quinn remembered that Balmer's house was close to the bus terminal. It was easy to find. The front yard, enclosed by a rusting chain-link fence, still had the look of a salvage yard: overturned wheelbarrow, ladders, derelict cement mixer with a wheel missing, bamboo poles for scaffolding, posthole diggers, odd lengths of PVC pipe. For the first time, Quinn began to see value in what he'd initially regarded as detritus.

The gate on the fence was secured with a heavy padlock. Quinn tried a key from the ring that seemed to match its size and heft, and it clicked open. The gate swung freely, and he threaded through the path Balmer had carved out to the front door. Quinn tried turning the knob before selecting another key and found it unlocked. He wondered where the dog was.

The building seemed to sag. Balmer's construction skills had not been invested in the house, which was sparsely furnished except for the shelves crammed with books. A recliner with cracks in the faux-leather upholstery sat in a corner where the light was good, and a square table with a single chair took up the center of the room. The piled invoices and papers and bottles of condiments suggested multi-use, dining room and office. In the middle of the table, secured by a border of duct tape, was a manila envelope bearing the inscription "Last Will and Testament of Roy Edward Balmer."

It contained a single typed page. The print was faint and hard to read, and some of the Os were inked in, suggesting that an old manual typewriter was somewhere about. But the will was legible enough. It directed cremation, as Quinn had somehow assumed was all right, and called for a "Buddhist, Christian interfaith service with internment of ashes at the Foreign Cemetery in Chiang Mai."

The bequest listed a bank account number and access code and directed that any remaining money be distributed to the Golden Triangle Education Fund. Quinn looked at the date under Balmer's steady signature. Today was May 15; the document was dated just a couple months earlier. The timing seemed odd, but Quinn figured Balmer must have been thinking about something. He folded the document in three, like a letter, and then in half so it fit in his shirt pocket. Maybe it was only that he was making a salary now and had something to give away.

Quinn poked around the house, mostly out of curiosity or maybe as another way of saying goodbye. The bedroom was squared away, ready for inspection, with an army cot neatly made. Out back was a *phi* house on a pole, dedicated to the land spirit to help keep evil away. Branches from a heavily laden orange tree in the next yard hung over the wall. Quinn picked a nice-looking orange and placed it in the spirit house as an offering to help Balmer on his way.

Back inside, Quinn scanned Balmer's library. Among the mysteries and thrillers was a copy of *The Asian Journal of Thomas Merton*, the book Balmer had told him about. He took it, thinking Balmer would be fine with that.

He caught the late afternoon bus, which he hoped would have him back in Chiang Mai in time for Happy Hour at the Gymkhana Club or the Press Club; he didn't care which. In the waiting room, he called Kay again and updated her.

"Found the will," he told her. "He wants an ecumenical service, Christian and Buddhist. Is that even possible?"

"The monks won't care. It's the Christians who might give us some grief. They're bible thumpers here, missionaries—Jesus's way or the highway. There's a guy who preaches Dudism; I'm sure he's available. The Chiang Mai Community Church has a Unitarian pastor. Maybe he'll do it. I'll check."

"Perfect. Roy said he wants his ashes placed in the Foreign Cemetery."

"And we can have the service there. They have a columbarium wall."

"Never noticed it."

"You have to look. And how about a reception at the club following the service? I'll ask Sarah Purcell to book the Leonowens Verandah. Outdoors would be nice." As usual, Kay was a few steps ahead of Quinn.

The bus ride to Chiang Mai would take half the time of the Fang leg. Better highway, fewer stops. Quinn perused a copy of the *Chiang Mai Mail* from the newsstand, reading the usual sensational stories—teenager stabs mother to death for refusing to give him money to buy lottery tickets, elderly monk trampled to death by wild elephant at forest monastery—and all the columns: "Care for Animals" (protect your dog from dehydration in the heat), "Doctor's Consultation" (home remedies for sciatica pain), and "Heart to Heart With Hillary" (helping infatuated *farangs* decide whether to marry a just-met bar hostess who seemed to really love them).

He did the Sudoku, Jumble, and crossword puzzles (he missed "reha," a four-letter word for "emu relative"). He skipped the horoscope but checked the classifieds to see what renting a better apartment on Nimanhaemin Road might cost. Reading the obituaries reminded him of one more thing he had to do. He had to find a suitable photograph of Balmer from the shots he had taken at Baan Nakha and Na Soi.

Quinn dozed until the cacophony of the Chiang Mai bus station jolted him awake. He was done in. Happy Hour anywhere was out of the question.

A dog barked in the courtyard when the tuk-tuk pulled up in front of the Damn Rat.

"Quiet, Hmah. It's all right," Quinn said softly. The pooch recognized him and approached with its tail wagging.

Quinn dropped his bag on the couch and sank down into it. He took out *The Asian Journal* and randomly picked a page. Merton was discussing Plutarch's notion of the blending of different spiritual beliefs into a harmonious One. If the Romans could mix Greek mythology with Christian dogma, Merton figured, the same should work with Hindus, Buddhists, Christians and Jains and Zoroastrians. Same same. He soon fell asleep, the open book covering him like a blanket.

163

CHAPTER EIGHTEEN

Memorial Service

A WEEK LATER, ROY'S ASHES arrived at the Damn Rat in a red-and-yellow DHL box. The package was heavier than Quinn had expected it would be, because the cremains were ensconced in a thick rosewood box.

Buddhist tradition calls for allowing time for a departed soul to migrate to its new life before a funeral service is held. Some believed that was a hundred days. Noi said the less orthodox Thais thought about a week was long enough. Since Balmer had made it sound as if he was being fast-tracked, Quinn opted for the shorter time frame. Working with Kay and Sarah Purcell, the Unitarian minister, and the Foreign Cemetery funeral director, he scheduled the memorial for the following Thursday. Noi had checked with a monk; it was an auspicious date.

On the morning of the ceremony, high, puffy cumulus clouds were drifting across the azure sky like ambling elephants. Attendance was greater than anyone had anticipated, and more folding chairs had to be brought from the storage shed. Among the congregation were members of the Gymkhana Club and the VFW, Ryder, and two other members of the Chiang Rai Outlaws, who rumbled up loudly. Several people turned around and looked their way, some with annoyance. Tee joined Quinn and Kay in the front row.

"I just talked to Roy a couple of weeks ago," he said. "He

was encouraging me about going back to school full time. Told me I was too smart for pounding nails."

When Major Purcell had sent out to the club membership his email announcing Balmer's "unfortunate and untimely" passing, he had requested that all the war veterans wear their uniforms, to honor his military service. Quinn was surprised so many showed up in peaked caps, Sam Browne belts, and green serge jackets complete with campaign medals.

Teddy Dingle was there too. For once he didn't try to make himself the life of the party or head to the front row. Quinn noticed he was moving slowly and gingerly, leaning heavily on a cane as he moved to the back.

A gong sounded, and the service began with a procession of three saffron-robed monks, slowly approaching a low riser set up in front of the columbarium wall. The senior monk blessed the crowd with holy water sprinkled from the brass bowl held by the second monk. Behind them, a young novice accepted offerings of marigolds and incense.

As the elder monk mounted the platform, the other two encircled the crowd of mourners with a white *sai sin* string. Quinn had read about that part of the ceremony. The string was to bind the community in prayer for the deceased's safe journey to the next incarnation. All three monks began chanting a series of low, slow funeral dirges. Quinn thought the chanting went on about as long as a sung high mass.

The Christian minister was a tall, ascetically lean American with an Amish beard, in mufti except for his Unitarian Universalist holy-chalice prayer shawl. Approaching the platform from his front-row seat, he bowed deeply to the senior monk, who returned the gesture with a perfunctory *wai*, like the kind of salute a colonel gives a private. There was no question who was in charge.

Reverend Ken, as he introduced himself, had turned around to face the audience.

"Can you hear me in back?" he asked in a reedy voice. A latecomer, someone in the last row, gave a thumbs up.

"I didn't know Roy Balmer," the Reverend began, commencing with a batch of well-intentioned platitudes. He told the congregants that Roy, from all he had heard, was a good man, had strong, inviolable principles, was in a better place now, safe from life's raging storms, so we should celebrate his life and not mourn its loss. And let his passing be a reminder of our own mortality and treasure "every living moment we're given on this little speck of dust in the universe we call Earth."

Better than nothing, Quinn thought.

Reverend Ken pulled a thin booklet from his breast pocket and said, "I would like to conclude with a prayer." Which he did, and which Quinn thought was pretty good too, covering the ashes to ashes, being born out of primal mud and now soaring on the astral plane. Just a few minutes more and he concluded, bowed to the monks again, and said "Amen."

There was nothing left to do but place the ashes in the columbarium niche and install the brass plaque with "Roy Edward Balmer, 1950-2013" that Quinn had had made. A cemetery worker with a bucket of mortar and a trowel was standing by.

But Quinn rose from his chair, holding the Merton book from Balmer's house.

"I would like to read a prayer as well, if I might," he said.

Reverend Ken looked to the senior monk, who nodded his assent.

Opening the book to a marked page, Quinn cleared his throat and said, "A Prayer for Peace." The Reverend perked up; he seemed familiar with the selection. The prayer was long and lyrical, more an ode than an invocation, evoking images of the fury of wars, the rise of empires, the smoke of their downfall; the fury of ten thousand fratricidal battles, and the desecration of science in creating horrific weapons of destruction. Quinn closed the book before reciting the last lines from memory:

> *"Lord, God,*
> *Grant us the peace*
> *To see your face*
> *In the darkest night.*
> *Teach us*
> *To seek peace and unity in*
> *This world and beyond.*
> *Show us how to love one another*
> *Across all borders,*
> *Races, cultures, philosophies, and religions.*
> *Amen."*

The service was over then, and as the crowd began to disperse, Kay took Quinn's arm.

"I loved the Merton prayer," she said, "especially the last lines. When did he write that?"

"Just now. I was only the courier."

Kay looked at him. She didn't hold Quinn's arm tighter, but she didn't let go, either.

The back gate of the cemetery, unlocked for the occasion, led onto the ninth fairway of the golf course. The congregants passed slowly through to the clubhouse for the reception. Duffers stopped mid-swing to pay respect by doffing their caps.

Quinn and Kay went inside to the bar and ordered a bottle of red wine. "It's going to be a long afternoon," Kay said.

The bar was getting stuffy. They collected the bottle and two glasses and walked out onto the Leonowens Verandah. Noi had insisted on catering the event and was supervising the serving line of hot dishes warmed by sterno candles.

"They kind of look like votive lights, don't you think?" said Quinn.

"No," Kay said.

"I'll join you two in a bit," Noi told them.

Moving across the Verandah and down its steps, they found an unoccupied table under the Gymkhana's majestic old rain tree, soaring more than sixty feet above them. Its thick green canopy and long, arching branches had provided welcome shade to club members for a hundred and fifty years.

In his role as VFW post commander, Bill Smith approached their table with a triangle-folded American flag in a glass display case.

"Here is the memorial flag for Veteran Balmer," he said. No one knew his rank.

Bill Smith presented the flag to Quinn with both hands, took a step back, and saluted.

"His country thanks him for his service."

Quinn didn't know the protocol and had never learned how to salute. He took the flag in his own two hands, gave a quick head bow, and placed the flag in its display case on the table next to a jar of cut marigolds.

"There's one more thing," Bill Smith said. "I remember how upset Roy was about the American kids left behind, the *luk kreung.*"

"He left a son behind in Vietnam."

"That's what I figured. There's a group in the States, in Colorado, I think, that's using DNA to make matches with the *bui doi* kids. In Vietnam and Thailand too. They have a big database. The consulate maybe can help."

"Too late. Roy is ashes now."

"Maybe not. They can trace DNA from bone fragments."

"Hold on," Quinn said, standing up. "I'll be right back."

He quick-marched through the back gate to the cemetery, where the worker with the trowel was just finishing sealing the niche. The cement wasn't yet dry.

Quinn ran up to him shouting, *"Hyud,"* the expression he used for getting tuk-tuks to stop. The cemetery manager heard him and rushed over. As Quinn explained, the manager shook his head briefly and then instructed the worker to undo his work. The worker shook his head too.

Retrieving the urn, Quinn carried it back to the table under the rain tree and said to Kay, "Maybe it isn't too late." He had told her about Balmer's son and his lingering sadness at having abandoned him. "Roy would want us to keep looking," he said.

"I know."

Bill Smith was still there. "Let us know if we can help," he told them. "Maybe we can."

He saluted again and went to join the other vets, one of them holding the trumpet for "Taps" at the end of the ceremony.

A few minutes later, Tee, who had jumped in to help at the bar, joined them. He looked surprised when he saw the urn on the table.

"Kuhn Roy," he said. "What is he doing here?"

"We want to do some DNA testing. Roy may have left a son behind in Vietnam."

"He told me about that when we were in the hill country. It still bothered him."

"Yes, it did."

"Do you need to get back right away?" Kay asked Tee. The bar line was down; only the committed drinkers were ordering one more.

"No, we're okay," Tee said.

"Listen, I know you're going to school in Bangkok in the fall, Tee, but we have a new project in Tak that Roy was going to head up."

"He told me about it."

"Any chance you could fill in until we find someone else?"

Tee glanced back at the bar. Quinn got it. It seemed like someone was always asking him to fill in.

"Maybe, *Kuhn* Kay. Okay. Let me finish out the semester here and tie up a few things. Can we talk about it then? The new term in Bangkok doesn't start until August."

Just then, someone Quinn thought he recognized came over to the table.

"Hi, Jane," said Kay. "Thanks for coming. You know Jane, don't you, Tee? Jack, this is Jane Harmon, our consul general."

That was it. Quinn recognized her from pictures in the society section of the *Chiang Mai Mail*. With her short graying hair, she appeared to be in her early fifties, and she had presence—an Eastern establishment, State Department look, Quinn thought. Maybe Yale; probably Harvard. She wore a smart tailored suit and was carrying a bag big enough to hold missile codes.

She shook hands with Quinn and then with Tee. "I'd heard about Mr. Balmer and his good work with your school projects. I wanted to be here."

Quinn saw an opportunity and seized it. "Consul General Harmon—"

"Jane."

"Jane. Roy may have left a son in Vietnam. I heard about possible DNA testing to look for a match...."

"You need to contact Dick Collins," Jane Harmon told him. "He's our citizen-services point man. He should be able to help."

Quinn noticed she didn't say he would be able to help.

Jane Harmon jotted down a number on the back of her business card.

"My private line," she said, handing it to Quinn. "Let me

know how it goes." Just then the cell phone in her bag rang. "On my way," she said, and then to Kay, "Have to go. Things may be heating up in Bangkok."

CHAPTER NINETEEN

Consular Affairs

Q UINN BROUGHT BALMER'S ASHES home to the Damn
Rat and put them back on his desk. He stared at the
box for a while and then opened it. Inside, with the
fine gray ash, were a few particles of bone. Grabbing a pair
of ice tongs from the kitchen, he gingerly extracted a piece.
A zip-lock plastic bag didn't seem a fitting repository for it,
but that was all he had.

Then he turned on his desktop computer and checked
the consulate website. Business hours were from nine until
five; it was just approaching four. He dialed the number and
a voice told him to push one for English, if he knew the
extension he could dial it at any time, and to listen carefully because the menu options had changed. There were
choices for passports (new or lost or stolen), Thai legal issues,
international drivers' licenses, and questions about Social
Security, Medicare, and veterans benefits.

Selecting the last option, he waited while the extension
rang and rang. No recording came on the line to tell him his
call was important or ask him to leave a message and we'll
get right back to you. Eventually, he was disconnected.

Quinn dutifully redialed, listened to the entire menu
again, and then got more vacant rings. He jabbed 0 for Oper-
ator. When that didn't work, he said, "Agent" repeatedly,
until he finally heard a sweet, live voice say "*Sawadee khap.*"

"Dick Collins, please," he said, trying to sound calm.

"Transferring." And she was gone before he could ask for the extension number in case the call was lost.

Another voice, sounding mildly annoyed, came on the line. "Collins."

"I'd like to make an appointment to discuss a VA issue."

"We do that Fridays."

"That's tomorrow."

"So it is."

Silence.

"What time is available?"

"Name it."

"Ten?"

"Okay. What's your name?"

"Quinn."

"First or last?"

"Last."

"What's your first?"

"Jack."

"You're on the schedule. Ten tomorrow. American time, not Thai time."

Collins chuckled. *Farangs* joked that Thais were habitu-ally late or didn't show up at all. Sometimes that was true, but Quinn thought it just showed that their culture didn't sweat the small stuff.

The next morning, Quinn put the coffee on and was in and out of the shower before the pot was done. The tuk-tuk ride to the consulate would take only ten minutes, twenty at most, if the morning commute was backed up on Prisani Road. It wasn't, and he arrived early.

The consulate building, a mid-century block of concrete behind a tall crenellated wall, had a certain ponderous, stark, almost Stalin-esque design element to it.

Quinn bypassed the long line of visa supplicants and went straight to the front gate. A Thai soldier in a shiny helmet spoke through a microphone from behind thick glass.

"Appointment?" he asked. Quinn gave his name. The guard scanned a list on a clipboard and said, "Mister Jack." He told him he was early and directed him to step aside. At precisely ten, he buzzed him into the building.

Quinn wondered where the United States Marines were. He had expected to see expeditionary forces in white hats, creased khaki shirts, and blue trousers with a long red stripe down the side. Then he spotted one behind the information desk in the lobby, scanning outside activity on a closed-circuit TV screen.

"Sir?" the young corporal said when he sensed Quinn's presence. No smile, and Quinn wondered why. Pretty good gig, he thought, consulate duty in Chiang Mai. There were much worse global deployments out there, Afghanistan and Iraq among them. Cheer up, Quinn thought.

"Veterans benefits," Quinn said.

"Fourth floor." The corporal pointed toward the elevator.

A notice on a bulletin board beside the up and down buttons was captioned PROTOCOL FOR AMERICAN INDE-PENDENCE DAY CELEBRATION (FOUR JULY). The notice, a full page, stated that "due to the threat of recent demon-stration activity in Thailand, this year's celebration at the consulate will be limited to American citizens only. We care about your safety!"

Phen and Kay had told Quinn that all the Thais they knew loved going to the Fourth of July event, the one time the Americans could reciprocate for the hospitality the Thais always showed them. While he waited for the slow elevator, Quinn unpinned the notice and stuffed it in his back pocket.

On the top floor, he found the Veterans Benefits office at the end of the hall. KNOCK BEFORE ENTERING, a sign on the door directed. When he did, he heard a squeaking desk chair, maybe being adjusted from recline to upright.

"Come!" bellowed a deep voice.

Quinn turned the knob, but the door was locked. He heard clumping footsteps, and then Dick Collins opened the door a crack.

"Yes?" he asked, eyeing Quinn.

"I'm your ten o'clock."

"Oh, yeah," Collins said. "Right on time." He undid the security latch and motioned Quinn to one of the chairs in front of a gray metal desk.

Collins's appearance didn't surprise Quinn. He wore a short-sleeved white shirt with a skinny black tie, and his worn leather belt showed expanded notches. He had a swirling eighties-style haircut, heavy on top, and a thick, dark moustache. Quinn guessed he was in his fifties, too old to be doing this kind of low-level administrative work, he thought. Collins certainly did not seem to be driving in the fast lane.

"How can I help?" asked Collins as he planted his ample posterior in his chair, tented his fingers, and leaned forward a bit to feign interest.

"I'm trying to locate the child of a Vietnam veteran."

"Asking for a friend, right? Don't worry, no judgments here!" His snigger put Quinn on edge.

"He is a friend. Was. Just died. Bill Smith from the VFW said there's a possibility of finding a match from a *bui doi* database."

"They're called *luk kreung* here." Collins seemed proud of himself for knowing that.

"I know."

"Yeah, there's a group in Colorado Springs. We got a few kits. You spit into a bottle." He reached into his desk drawer and tossed Quinn a padded, postage-paid envelope. "We still get a few vets looking for their kids, even after all these years."

"Bill said something about DNA from bone fragments."

"Bill's always up to something. Always finding more things

for me to do, bless his heart. You should hear him go on about Agent Orange and disability for the Air Force guys that served here. That's going nowhere. Look, we don't do bones."

He picked up some papers from his overflowing in-box— not much was in the out—and the conversation appeared to be over.

Quinn thought Roy deserved better. So he changed tack. Luffed the sails and then billowed the spinnaker. He rocked forward and pulled the Fourth of July notice out of his back pocket.

"What is this all about?" he asked.

"Can't be too careful."

"About what?"

"Increased Red Shirt or some such demonstrations in Bangkok. Our political guys say it may be headed this way. Why don't you let us suss this out?"

"Who? You and Daryl Kerwin?"

"You know Daryl?"

"Yes."

"Can't comment. That's classified."

"Maybe I'll call Jane Harmon."

"So you know Consul General Harmon too. You get around."

"Chiang Mai is a pretty small town."

"Well, you go ahead and do what you need to do."

Collins pushed himself up from his desk, marched to the office door, and opened it quickly. And slammed it hard when Quinn had barely cleared it.

Quinn hadn't really planned on calling Jane Harmon, but by the time he got back down to the lobby, he was still fuming over Collins's dismissive attitude—whether about the DNA test or the Fourth of July, he wasn't sure. He paused before a rack of government pamphlets on subjects like avoiding email scams, how to vote absentee, and the benefits of daily exercise even if for only twenty minutes. He considered his options for a moment. Then, retrieving Jane Harmon's business card from his wallet, he dialed her number.

"It's Jack Quinn."

"Jack," she said. "What's up?"

"Sorry to bother you, Jane. I just met with Dick Collins."

"And how did that go?"

"He didn't seem particularly interested in helping with the DNA testing for Roy."

"Ah, Dick. Bless his heart. Never breaks a sweat. But look, the consulate in Ho Chi Minh City has some good forensic guys. Get me a sample of Roy's DNA, and we'll follow up. There's a group in the States that links G.I. dads and their kids left behind."

"They're still making matches?"

"Still are."

"Wars never end, I guess."

Quinn felt surprised and gratified by her response. He decided to push his luck.

"Thank you, Jane," he said. "One more thing?"

"Shoot."

"I saw the notice in the lobby about the Fourth of July celebration this year. No Thai guests?"

"Oh, that. Yes, I just found out about it. Sometimes the fellas get a little ahead of themselves. They love this cloak-and-dagger stuff. But look, no worries. The party is going on as usual. The notice is coming down."

"Skip the one in the lobby. I already got it."

"Thanks. I've always appreciated citizen action."

KAY HAD SUGGESTED QUINN take a few days off after the funeral, but he told her he thought it'd be better if he worked. Early the following morning, he stopped by Sweetie Pie on the way to the office. Noi had not yet arrived. He

180

stepped behind the counter and poured himself a cup of coffee, something all the regulars did. Next to the cash register was a stack of that morning's *Chiang Mai Mail.*

Quinn grabbed a paper and took his usual table by the front window, where he could watch the day unfold. After taking a sip of his coffee, he opened the *Mail* and found a front-page story with the headline "Independence Day Celebration at the American Consulate On as Usual."

He took another swallow of coffee and read the article, which said in part, "Late yesterday afternoon, Consul General Jane Harmon announced that the popular Independence Day celebration at the American consulate on Witchayanon Road will take place as scheduled on July Fourth from noon until dark. There had been reports that due to security concerns, the event might be canceled or attendance limited. The Honorable Mrs. Harmon told the *Mail*, 'I don't know where those stories came from. We feel very safe and secure here among our Thai friends and neighbors. Independence and friendship are values both our countries share, and we want to ensure the tradition of the Independence Day celebration continues on as always.' Admission is free."

The door opened and Noi walked in, lugging plastic string bags filled with fresh produce from the morning market.

"Hi, Jack," she said. "Nice service for Roy."

She plopped the bags on the counter and came back with a fresh pot of coffee to give Quinn a refill. As she poured, Quinn pointed to the story in the *Mail* and asked, "Ever been?"

"Never miss it. Everyone goes."

"Really?"

"We love it. Shows us you Americans know how to do *sanuk*. Have a little fun. Live in the moment," she added as she headed back to the kitchen.

Quinn took a few more sips while flipping through the

Mail, then folded it up and shouted to Noi, "Off to work."

"So soon?"

"Life goes on, I guess."

"It does, *Khun* Jack."

Quinn got to the GTEF office at nine, just as Kay was opening the door.

"You're early, Jack," she said. Quinn usually rolled in closer to ten. "You look like a commuter with that newspaper tucked under your arm."

"Have you seen this?" He showed her the story in the *Mail*.

"You can always count on Jane," Kay said. "How did the meeting with Dick Collins go?"

"Not so well. He's a prick."

"I could have told you that."

CHAPTER TWENTY

Elvis Has Left the Building

QUINN ALMOST TRIPPED OVER something on his doorstep as he set off to work one morning a few days later. It was a small macaque in a cage, looking annoyed. The fact of the monkey sitting there was strange enough. The fact that it was dressed in a sequined jumpsuit was stranger still. The cage had a small nameplate, and Quinn bent down to read it. "Elvis," it said.

What is going on? Quinn wondered. I have enough on my plate, and now, for some reason, here's Elvis. He took his own cleansing breath and decided to go with the flow.

Quinn had read about Elvis the monkey in the "What's On" section of the *Chiang Mai Mail*. Graceland, a club that featured Elvis Presley impersonators, as well as the odd Tom Jones and Englebert Humperdinck, had just opened on Loi Kroh Road. The Thais still loved Elvis Presley, the story explained, because he had invited King Bhumibol and Queen Sirikit onto the set of *G.I. Blues* during a state visit in 1960. Elvis the monkey was this Graceland's greeter.

Quinn carried the cage into his apartment and refilled the monkey's water bottle, which was getting low. Elvis must have been out there for a while. He called Kay to say he would be late getting in and why.

"What?"

"Exactly."

Set between the Kit Kat and Happy Home hostess bars,

the latter already open and blaring disco, Graceland still had its CLOSED sign in the window. But the front door was unlocked, and as soon as Quinn let himself in, he saw the owner of the place, looking sort of like the young Elvis himself with his slicked-back ducktail pompadour and gold-framed dark glasses.

"You found him!" he cried.

Just then out of the shadows strode Colonel Prasong Wongsarat.

"We have to stop meeting like this, *Khun* Jack," he said.

"I didn't take the monkey."

"I know that. We got it all on CCTV. Want to see?"

The surveillance tape showed a stooped, aging, noticeably limping man taking Elvis from his spot by the door.

"Recognize him?"

"You know I do, Prasong. It's Teddy Dingle."

"Bingo! Mr. Law and Order himself. Look, he's almost posing for the camera. It's like he wants to be caught."

"Why would Teddy Dingle steal a monkey?"

"That's for you to figure out. He wants to talk to you. He says you're a lawyer."

"I'm not.... Never mind, where is he?"

"Provincial Remand Prison, out in Mae Tang."

PROVINCIAL REMAND WAS A sprawling new fortress that was built like an American Supermax, with thick concrete walls and slits instead of windows. At the sally-port entrance, Quinn was frisked, metal-detected, and ID'd. Once inside, he found Teddy at the back of a holding pen filled with rough-looking characters all jockeying for their few inches of turf.

When Teddy saw Quinn, he shuffled forward, momentarily granted deferential passage by his cellmates. When he reached Quinn, he held onto the cell bars like he was the monkey in a cage.

Teddy had never been one to care much about his appearance, but he looked particularly disheveled that morning. His thinning hair was flying wild, and the white stubble on his chin showed he hadn't shaved for a few days. He was dressed in an orange T-shirt and sagging maroon prison-issue below-the-knee shorts. He had no shoes, only flip-flops that showed ugly white feet.

"Why'd you put the monkey on my porch, for Chrissakes?"

"I thought maybe you could help. I saw how much you did for Tee."

"Tee's a friend," Quinn said, immediately regretting it. He didn't think Teddy could look any more abject, but that statement seemed to crush him. "Shit, Teddy. What were you thinking?"

"The old bones are giving out, I'm afraid. The docs at Chiang Mai Ram tell me I need a new hip or I won't be walking much longer."

Privately run and highly regarded, Chiang Mai Ramkhamhaeng Hospital was where foreigners went for surgery, nips-and-tucks, and dental implants.

"Can't afford it. Finances are running low. Got another rent rise. Have you checked food prices at Tesco Lotus lately? I need to go home, Quinn. The National Health will take care of me when I get back to England. Maybe they'll find me some council housing up in Spennymoor."

"Things are as bad as all that?"

"Worse."

"But a monkey?"

"I figured they'd nab me and deport me as a no-account, like they do sometimes. Send me home as an undesirable."

"That was the plan?"

"It was the best I could come up with. Thought it was worth a try."

"Why didn't you contact the British consulate?"

"They weren't very sympathetic. They seem to find me difficult, for some reason."

"Really. Okay, let me see what I can do. Is there anything you need?"

Teddy looked around the cell. "I need everything," he said.

As he left, Quinn pondered what to do, then decided to stop by the Gymkhana Club. Maybe Clive Purcell would be willing to help a compatriot in distress.

The Major was on duty, at his post behind his office door. Quinn knocked.

"Come through!" shouted the Major.

Quinn could see he was putting bar chits into neat piles.

"Ah," he said when Quinn entered. He could see the Major was trying to recall something. "How's the family?" he asked after a brief pause.

"Great, thanks. But I'm afraid I have to ask a favor."

"What is it now?"

"Teddy Dingle needs help."

"Wondering about that. Haven't seen him here in seems like donkey's years. His membership has lapsed, by the way. Need to mention that to him."

"He's in jail."

"Dingle? In jail? He cadges the occasional drink, leaves worthless chits," he looked at the pile on his desk, "but I'd never suspect him of criminal activity."

"He's in rough shape. Needs a new hip he can't afford. Rent rise; he's being turned out on the street." Quinn figured a little embellishment wouldn't hurt. "So he stole Elvis, the monkey from Graceland."

The Major looked so perplexed, Quinn backtracked with an explanation of Graceland's niche market in the entertainment industry.

"Well, we've noticed Dingle's behavior becoming increasingly bizarre of late, now that you mention it. Nothing serious, but his comments, especially to the ladies, are becoming more offensive, and he's getting increasingly peevish as well. Fits of anger. But why in God's name would he steal a monkey?"

"To get caught. He thinks he'll be deported and the British government will have to pay his way home. He's not thinking straight."

"Why doesn't he contact the consulate? Oh, wait. I've heard he may be persona non grata there. Well, we have to do something for him, I suppose. Can't have our chaps going around stealing monkeys."

"How about a fundraiser?"

"He doesn't have many friends, to be honest. In fact, a lot of people can't stand him. I can put a squib in the next newsletter, I suppose."

"That's the best you can do?"

"Off the top of my head. I will phone the consulate, of course. Can't have our chaps going around stealing monkeys," he repeated.

"You're a brick, Major."

Quinn had heard the Brits say that to each other in times like these. The Major shot a cuff and looked at his watch.

"Must get back to business," he said, returning to his bookkeeping.

Teddy Dingle's preliminary hearing was set for two weeks later. In the meantime, Quinn made regular visits to the prison, bringing him rations of Vienna sausage and Cadbury chocolate bars as requested. He always stayed to watch Teddy eat the food he had brought, afraid that it might be taken from him.

One afternoon, Quinn stopped by Sweetie Pie to talk to Bill Smith and the other vets. He told them Teddy had done some World War II home service, and Bill agreed to put a donation jar on their table.

"Anything for a vet," he said.

You never saw Noi frown, Quinn thought, but she did when he asked for another jar by the cash register. She paused, ignoring the order-up bell.

"Of course," she said after a moment. "Do you have a picture of him?"

"I don't."

AT THE HEARING, QUINN was permitted to sit at the defense table, because Colonel Prasong had told the court he was a lawyer.

The judge hearing Teddy's case was not as amiable as Judge Verapol Tungsawan had been when he'd let Tee slide in the queen's-head case. The Honorable Somchai Suttirat sat behind a towering bench, peering down from under scales of justice balanced on the hilt of a royal sword. Her eyes were piercing as she made it clear she was not going to brook any nonsense. After hearing the young prosecutor read the charges, she asked Teddy, through the court interpreter, to stand and plead.

"Guilty with circumstances, My Lord," Teddy said.

The interpreter struggled to find the right Thai words.

"Let's do this in English to save everyone time," the judge said to the prosecutor. "Is that all right with you?"

The prosecutor nodded.

"There is no such thing as guilty with circumstances in Thailand, Mr. Dingle, and I'm not your lord," the judge said.

"Very good, ma'am," Teddy said obsequiously, pronouncing it *marm*. Quinn gently guided him back into his seat.

"What are you recommending?" the judge asked the prosecutor.

"Mr. Dingle has been in the kingdom for several years, Your Honor, and this is his first offense. But the monkey was very valuable to the owner, personally and to his livelihood."

The judge rolled her eyes.

"This is grand larceny, Your Honor," the prosecutor persisted. "We're proposing six months in jail, with time served."

"He stole a monkey, for Buddha's sake. He didn't hurt it and left it where it would be found. Here's the deal, Mr. Dingle. I read the probation report. You're facing financial difficulties, it seems, and some health issues as well. The court is sympathetic to your situation. But, we're sorry, it's time for you to go home."

Teddy sighed with audible relief. "Love to. Except I don't have the fare."

"Well, we're not in the travel business here. Time served plus sixty days, but as soon as you get the money together for a ticket, you're free to go. Home. And not come back. Fair enough?"

"Yes, Your Honor," Teddy said.

"Yes, Your Honor," Quinn affirmed.

As soon as the judge left the bench and court was no longer in session, Teddy slumped into his chair. What little wind he'd had left in him was gone. The thought of more time in a Thai jail seemed more than he could handle. Quinn put his hand on his knee.

"We'll get the money," he said.

But he didn't know how. The cheapest fare from Bangkok's Suvarnabhumi International Airport to Gatwick was five hundred dollars. Total donation receipts from all sources to date was less than a hundred. Quinn checked the donation jars daily, and the trickle had stopped.

"I sent off the notice to the publicity committee," said the Major when Quinn called him. "Mrs. Purcell said the next newsletter will be out in a week, maybe."

Things weren't looking promising.

"Maybe I can help, *Kuhn* Jack," Phen said as they were discussing the situation at the office. "Tee told me about it."

"You know Tee?"

"We had a few classes together at CMU."

"Oh. Well, we're running out of options."

"Let's try GoFundMe. It's all the rage here. I'll put up a page and share it with friends. I'll say we can help a kindly *farang* grandpa who's *mai di*, not well. They'll respond."

"You would do that knowing what he did to Tee? Why?"

"Score me some karma? Man?" She flashed a peace sign. And a smile.

Less than a week later, Quinn was back at the prison.

"You have enough to fly Emirates, Business Class," he told Teddy. "You're going home."

CHAPTER TWENTY-ONE

Back at the Press Club

TWO WEEKS LATER, PHEN called over to Quinn. *"Kuhn Jack, it's Tee on the line."*

Quinn grabbed the phone, as did Kay from upstairs. "What's up, Tee?" she asked.

"I'm ready to talk about the Tak project with you. Any chance we can meet tonight? How about at the Press Club?"

"Great, Tee. We're getting some pressure from the Commission to start."

When Quinn and Kay walked into the Press Club after work, Tee was already sitting at the bar. As they grabbed two more stools, Quinn noticed, for the first time since he had been coming to the Press Club, that Derek was not at his post behind the bar.

"Where's Derek?" he asked Mayuri, the bartender.

"Sanuk," she replied. Quinn understood that in this instance, the word meant "vacation." *"Nit noi,"* she added— he won't be gone long.

"Derek doesn't seem like a week at Koh Samui type," Quinn said.

"He's not," Kay said.

"Where, then?"

"Okay, Jack, going out on a limb a bit by telling you this. He's in Burma."

"What, now? Why?"

Kay looked up at the poster of Aung San Suu Kyi, still in

its prominent place behind the bar.

"Derek's an old soldier. He's still fighting. Been supporting Aung and the pro-democracy folks for years."

"Which means what, exactly?"

"The military has shut down all communication inside Burma: cell phones, internet. Derek sneaks information in on thumb drives to spread the word to the democracy supporters. He bucks them up with news about international support for Aung."

"I just read that the Burmese Air Force, such as it is, is bombing Karen villages," Tee added. "The tribes support Aung too."

"Still can't feature old Derek in dark glasses and a trench coat," said Quinn.

"He's one of those old lefties who never quit," Kay told him. "He hates colonialism and military dictatorships. Sometimes I think it's fighting back that keeps him alive."

"Derek gave me a copy of *The Quiet American*, Graham Greene, a while ago," Tee said. "Said it was all I needed to know about colonialism in Southeast Asia."

"So how does Derek's scheme work, exactly?" asked Quinn, intrigued.

"Derek has a few runners, older Americans and Brits cut from the same cloth."

Quinn sat straighter at the bar, and Tee leaned in closer. Kay switched to sotto voce, the way Derek would have had he been there.

"There's a town called Mae Sai on the northwest border. It's right across the river from the Burmese town of Tachileik. Horrible little place. But old expats bus up there, play a cheap round of golf at the Chinese resort, gamble at the casino, and pick up their black-market drugs. You know, now that I think about it, Jack, you'd fit the profile Derek is looking for."

For a second, Quinn saw the screaming face of a Karen guerrilla. "I think I'll pass for now," he said.

Kay shrugged. "So," she went on, "the runner goes to Tachileik, hangs around the market for a while, buys some black-market Viagra from a street vendor, and then heads to the Great Dagon Pagoda, like he's a tourist. The temple sits on a high hill just outside downtown. It's a long enough walk that you can see if anybody is following you. Derek says the Security Police, in orange vests and fake Ray-Bans, on motor bikes, are everywhere.

"Our guy walks onto the temple grounds. If the coast is clear, he goes to a monk standing by a well and pretends to ask for a blessing. When the monk obliges, he hands him a wad of money. Wrapped inside is the thumb drive. If anyone approaches, the monk drops it down the well. No one's been caught yet."

"So that's where Derek is now?"

"It's his first run in a while."

Just then, Colonel Prasong Wongsarat strolled through the front door.

"Ah, three of my favorite people!" he exclaimed. Still using English, he asked Mayuri, "And where might Mr. Davies be, *Khun* Mayuri?"

"*Mai lu*, don't know," she replied, polishing a glass that didn't need it. She went to the end of the bar to take an order that had already been placed.

"Thanks for the information," the Colonel said, and then, turning to Tee, "Keeping your nose clean, *Kuhn* Tuanthon? Staying out of trouble?"

"You know me, Colonel."

"Yes, I do. And here's a bit of friendly advice. I'd stay away from Bangkok for a while. Gotta run," he added, glancing at a watch that might have been a Rolex. "See you around."

"So when can you leave for Tak?" Quinn asked Tee as they

watched the Colonel head out the door.

"Give me a couple of days."

"Perfect," Kay said. "You'll go to the Viang Hotel in Tak City. Lots of NGO kids hang out there. The Commission is expecting you."

"What was the name of the hotel?"

"The Viang." Tee whipped out his cell phone and searched the internet. "Looks good," he said.

"Two and a half stars. You're booked under GTEF."

"Perfect."

"We'll tell them you're on your way," Quinn said as he handed over a set of rolled-up blueprints. "You'll find this easier than the work in Baan Nakha. Simpler plan, and you'll have more help. It'll go a lot faster."

"If I run into any trouble," Tee said a little sadly, "I'll ask myself what *Khun* Roy would do."

All three were quiet for a moment.

"Thank you, Tee," said Kay, and she hugged him.

"Thanks, Tee," Quinn echoed.

"Thanks, *Khun* Jack, *Khun* Kay. We'll do a good job on the new school."

Tee saluted them with the plans. Then, echoing the Colonel, he said, "Gotta run. I'll let you know when we get started."

The club was well into Happy Hour, and the dancing was about to begin. Mayuri started the set with a thumping "Proud Mary."

"Left a good job in the city," Tina Turner sang.

"Time to move?" Kay asked.

"Where to?" Quinn assumed she was thinking of calling it a day.

"The reading room?"

Quinn liked the sound of that. He held up two fingers to signal Mayuri it was time for another round. She gave him a thumbs up and rapped the bar twice.

When they were settled in the room's deep, comfortable chairs, Kay said, "I've been thinking about my Buddha head."

"You're still going to return it, right?"

"Right. Only now I've got some urgency. I'll have to move out of the Bunsho Mansions when Daryl splits. Before that, the Buddha needs to go home."

"Has he gotten his new assignment yet? Did Baghdad come through?"

"He's not Baghdad material. They told him he can have one of the 'stans—maybe Uzbekistan. He's still lobbying for Ukraine, but that doesn't seem to be going anywhere."

Quinn remembered Daryl lurking about the apartment like a ghost.

"Are you going to be all right, Kay?" he asked.

"Financially, you mean? Sure. Neither of us will contest the divorce; we always traveled light, not a lot of stuff to fight over. It'll be easy. I'll get one of those new condos on Nimanhaemin, close to Noi."

"The foundation can't pay very much."

"I'll get something out of the settlement, and I have a little inheritance money socked away. Old tobacco money. I'll be fine."

"I know you will, Kay."

"I'm going to take the Buddha head to Bangkok next week. To Wat Traimit, a thirteenth-century temple. It's the perfect final resting place. Want to come along?"

"What about Sukhothai?"

"Too late for that. And Wat Traimit has a program for artifact returns. They're looking for lost heads. It was in the *Post*."

"But isn't Bangkok dangerous right now, with all the protests?"

"The papers always make things sound worse than they are. There's always demonstrations about something, and anyway, it's only for one night. We'll be fine."

Quinn figured it had to be less risky than going to Burma like Derek. "Okay," he said. "I'll go."

He wasn't sure she heard him, though. Quinn could see Kay was drifting into some sort of reverie. She even closed her eyes.

"Tee mentioned Graham Greene's *The Quiet American*," she said when she came back around a few moments later. "It got me thinking about the Oriental Hotel in Bangkok. The place was built in 1876, the first Western hotel in Siam— low slung, with verandahs, right on the river. The original hotel is now the Authors' Wing. Daryl and I stayed there one night during happier times. Greene stayed there; so did Somerset Maugham."

"Teddy Dingle told me Maugham visited Chiang Mai in the twenties. He even played snooker in the billiards room at the club."

"Even Teddy got some things right on occasion. Maugham didn't like Chiang Mai, and liked Bangkok even less. He almost died from malaria on that trip. He wrote about it in *A Gentleman in the Parlour*. But I'm planning to stay at the old Royal Hotel, built in the thirties to cater to intrepid British travelers sampling exotic Asia. Very elegant for the day. And its location is great, close to the Royal Palace and the temples. You'll love it."

They fell into a few moments of easy silence, listening to the changeover to reggae and watching people bop toward the dance floor. When Bob Marley started "Jammin," Kay's friend Jerry came over, as he had on their previous visit.

"How about it, Kay?" he asked, nodding his head toward the dancers.

"You bet," she said.

CHAPTER TWENTY-TWO

Bangkok

"**P**HEN, CAN YOU MAKE Jack and me reservations for a flight to Bangkok, and for one night at the Royal?" Kay asked her assistant the next morning.

"Is that a good idea, *Kuhn* Kay? They say there's more trouble down there."

"We'll be okay. Like I told Jack, this stuff happens all the time. Anyway, we'll be flying into DMK," she reminded Phen. Don Muang was the old downtown airport, now used only for domestic flights. The sprawling new Suvarnabhumi International Airport was a likelier setting for protests.

Quinn envisioned the Royal Hotel, with its nearby temples and palaces and many, many tourists. "We won't be anywhere close to the protests," he added. He looked at Kay for confirmation but didn't get it.

Phen made the reservations, and at the end of the week, Quinn and Kay checked in at Nok Air for a late-afternoon flight from Chiang Mai. The baggage screener spotted the Buddha head in Kay's carry-on, but didn't stop the line or tell her to step aside. In fact, he *waied* deeply, as if a Buddha head in someone's luggage was something he saw every day.

There was nothing out of the ordinary on the taxi ride from the airport to the hotel, a curving, streamlined 1930s art moderne structure not far from the Royal Palace. The lobby featured a sweeping staircase perfect for the pre-World War II, European Cook's Tour crowd to descend in tuxedos and formal dresses for cocktails before dinner in the main salon.

The place had declined over time, though, and fallen into a state of almost benign shabbiness. The carpeting was worn, the chandeliers needed dusting, and the furniture sagged, like the aging budget travelers who sat on it. Rather than formal dinner jackets, the men wore safari shirts and shorts that showed their wrinkled knees.

"Could be Raffles in Singapore," Quinn imagined.

"The Strand in Rangoon," Kay said, playing along.

They did not descend the grand staircase arm in arm that evening. Kay had reserved a top-floor suite with a view of the Grand Palace, with its imposing European architecture and soaring Thai roof, and the phantasmagorical temples surrounding it. As they watched the sun set over the glistening temples, they ate two orders of tiger prawns with green chili sauce and drank a couple bottles of Singha.

"That's Wat Phra Kaew, the Temple of the Emerald Buddha," said Kay, pointing. "That one's Wat Pho, the Temple of the Reclining Buddha. Wat Arun, the Temple of Dawn, is across the river."

"And where are we taking the Buddha head?"

"Wat Traimit? It's down the road."

After a restless night's sleep from the noise of the constant traffic, Quinn was jolted awake by Kay's insistent knocking.

"We have to get an early start," she said in response to Quinn's groan at the door. "Beat the heat. It's a good long walk to the temple. I'll meet you in the lobby."

Kay handed Quinn the Buddha head, wrapped in a towel in her tote, when he offered to carry it.

Wat Traimit was down Yaowarat Road, a main street that curved like a dragon through a warren of lanes in Chinatown. To reach it, they had to pass the Phan Fa Lilat Bridge, which crossed the Lamphu Klong. To their surprise, demonstrators carrying signs were blocking the approach to the bridge. Several of the placards shouted "Democracy Now!" in English for the benefit of the foreign camera crews. The students were boisterous but not threatening. Even so, Quinn heard screaming police sirens, and they were getting louder.

"Step it up," Kay said urgently to Quinn, who had lingered to watch. "It doesn't look good."

"Didn't expect to see this," Quinn said. "Should we turn back?"

"We've come this far. Let's keep going."

Wat Traimit was just inside Chinatown's red pagoda gate. There, everything was quiet. Though it was early, a batch of tourists hoping to get a glimpse of the temple's five-ton, solid-gold Buddha were jammed at the entrance.

"Locked," bellowed an aggressively participating Elderhostel type. "Just talked to the head monk. The place is locked down because of the demonstrations. After we came all the way here."

The tourists started grumbling about the day's itinerary being blown all to hell. The Europeans flipped through their guidebooks to find alternatives. The Japanese tour guides lowered their follow-me flags.

"Let's try this way," Kay said, leading Quinn along the outside wall of the temple compound. A quarter-block down, they came to a narrow, unmarked door. After edging through, they climbed a set of steep wooden steps that led to the temple cloisters.

Kay knocked randomly on a door and someone answered from inside.

"*Yakh dai*? What do you want?" There was no beatific smile or sign of enlightened demeanor on the face of the old monk who opened the door a crack.

That changed immediately when Quinn opened Kay's bag. As soon as he looked inside, the monk *waied* deeply at the Buddha head and opened the door all the way. Reverently, he lifted the head from the bag and placed it on an altar behind a row of burning joss sticks. After mumbling a brief incantation in a low, throaty tone, he turned to them and began speaking in Thai.

Kay recognized one word. *"Tammai,* why?"

"Pai bahn," said Kay. "He needs to come home."

The monk nodded, as if he understood and there was nothing left to say. As if a tiny part of the universe had been put back into balance. As it should be. So be it. The monk handed each of them a temple amulet on a gold chain, blessed them, and watched as they went on their way.

As soon as they left the *wat,* they heard the pop of what sounded like gunfire and saw heavy smoke rising from the direction of the Royal Hotel. After passing the Fa Lilat Bridge again, they approached the winged Democracy Monument, the site of demonstrations against military coups since 1932, when the country had become a constitutional monarchy.

The situation had deteriorated from earlier in the day. Army troops in full battle gear had cordoned off the monument and were wading into the throng of protestors. The soldiers fired tear-gas canisters to disperse the crowd, and those who could not flee quickly enough were struck with rifle butts and batons. The injured and detained were roughly thrown into the armored personnel carriers standing by.

When they got back to the hotel, they were shocked to see the lobby had been turned into an aid station, with students in Red Cross vests tending to the injured. Wounds were bandaged, eyes irrigated, terrorized students comforted.

"I have some first-aid skills," Kay said as she moved forward to help.

"Me too," said Quinn. But they weren't needed; the students had the situation well in hand. "Maybe I can help get the kids out of jail," he said as they watched several soldiers frog-walking demonstrators into police vans. "Once an attorney—"

"We shouldn't stay here," Kay told him. As if that were a choice. As soon as they finished packing their bags, a soldier in black Kevlar gear was banging on doors.

"*Pai reou*! Time to go!" he yelled. "Now!" He led them and a few tourists from other rooms down the stairs—the elevators were no longer working—to pandemonium in the lobby.

The soldier led the evacuated hotel guests, looking more like an apocalyptic tour group, down Thanon Rachini Road to the National Museum. Once the residence of princes and retainers, it now housed the country's finest art treasures. The building had been left untouched, while nearby buildings had been tagged with freedom slogans and had their windows smashed. The soldier nodded briefly and walked away.

"What do we do now?" Quinn asked once they were on their own.

"The river."

The whole group trooped to the Phra Chan pier, on the Chao Phraya, to wait for a high-speed, long-tail water taxi. Quinn looked at his essentials-only overnight bag.

"I feel like a refugee," he said.

"You are," Kay told him. "We'll go to the Oriental. We'll be safe there."

The water-taxi driver demanded five-hundred *baht* for the short ride down the river.

"Surge pricing, I guess," Kay said, but she didn't try to bargain. Nor did the others in their panicked cohort, who shoveled piles of *baht* into the open hands of the crew.

Rooster tail shooting high from the stern, the boat sped off. Most of the passengers got off at the first stop, the Mahraj pier, on the Thon Buri side of the river, away from the violence. But Quinn and Kay remained on board until they got to the Oriental's pier, a few more stops down the river.

A worried-looking bellman in crisp white livery with gold piping assisted them off the boat and tentatively led them across the expansive front lawn. He took them past the original two-story hotel, now the Authors' Wing, to the lobby of the thirty-story tower looming behind it. Guests didn't usually arrive by boat, and the front-desk receptionist seemed dubious about Quinn and Kay's sweaty and wind-blown appearance.

"I'm so sorry," she said, glancing at Quinn's scruffy bag. "Fully booked."

"What about the Authors' Wing?" Kay asked.

"That's quite expensive, ma'am." The receptionist had obviously dealt with lots of low-ball *farangs* better suited to places like the Royal.

"The Somerset Maugham Suite," Kay said, slapping her Platinum credit card down.

"How many nights, *Kha?*"

By the time the charge on the card cleared, smiles and *wais* had ensued. The receptionist summoned the bellhop from the pier, who had been standing by, patient and vigilant. He took charge of the luggage and turned to retrace their path.

As they walked back to the Authors' Wing, Kay said to Quinn, "The Maugham Suite is the best. The Graham Greene Suite is austere, and the Joseph Conrad Suite is haunted." She seemed to want to push aside the day's violence. "Everyone stayed here back in the day."

Quinn confirmed that fact by reading aloud the honor roll of former guests, in the foyer. It included Leo Tolstoy, Victor Hugo, Rudyard Kipling, Oscar Wilde, George Orwell, and, he noted, Henrik Ibsen. Quinn could hear Thom Manderly projecting to the back of the theater at the Redbarn Playhouse. "Pear! Pear!"

The bellman led them to the second floor, unlocked the

door to Maugham Suite, stepped inside, and drew back the curtains. He opened French doors that led to a balcony with a view of the river. To Quinn, the traffic seemed heavy but not panicked.

"That was frightening," Kay said as soon as the bellman left, silently closing the door behind him. "I never expected it." She held up her right hand, watching it tremble a bit.

Quinn put on what he hoped was a brave face. "We can still leave tomorrow."

"Definitely," Kay said, as they both began to relax.

Looking around, Quinn thought that might be partly due to the suite. The high ceilings were studded with reflecting glass stars, and the walls were awash with pink and maroon silk coverings. The bedroom had canopied beds.

"Looks a little bordelloish," he observed. "Not that I'm complaining."

"Maybe they thought it's what Maugham would have wanted. More likely, he was looking for a little comfort. He'd just come off a six-month overland trek from Ceylon. He'd crossed Burma on ponies."

"Comfort he got," Quinn said as he ducked his head into the bathroom, which was dominated by a mammoth free-standing tub with gold fitments.

The sitting room contained a complete library of Maugham's works. Kay ran a finger along the leather-bound set, looking for something.

"Here it is, *The Gentleman in the Parlour*," she said as she began flipping through the pages. "It's about his stay in Thailand in the 1920s." She found the page she was looking for and read, "'I lay there panting and sleepless, and shapes of monstrous pagodas and great gilded Buddhas bore down on me. These wooden rooms with verandahs make every sound frightfully audible to my tortured ears.' He wrote that here, in this room. He'd come down with malaria and had

209

a temperature of a hundred and five degrees. They didn't think he'd make it.

"Oh, look, Graham Greene," she said, noticing a book on a table, possibly left behind by a previous guest. She handed Quinn a copy of *The Quiet American.*

"Derek's book."

Kay nodded. "My favorite character is Phuong, the beautiful young Vietnamese woman that Pyle, the young CIA guy, falls in love with. It's something about how she's tougher than we'll ever be. She'll get old but won't ever be obsessed with arrogance and false ideals, like we are. You should read it."

"Maybe I should."

Now that Quinn had a moment to breathe, he realized he was famished. They hadn't eaten since early morning.

"Lord Jim's," Kay said when he mentioned it. "The restaurant here."

Lord Jim's sported a nautical theme, but to Quinn's mind it suggested Scott Fitzgerald more than Joseph Conrad. Yacht club burgees were strung from the ceiling; crossed oars polished to a high sheen hung on the wall. Snappy navy-blue-striped duck fabric covered the chairs and banquettes. Borneo was nowhere to be seen.

The waiter brought them gargantuan leather-covered menus. "What's good?" Quinn asked Kay.

"It's the Oriental. Everything is good." She seemed as distracted as Quinn felt.

Quinn went Western with herb-encrusted rack of lamb. Kay stayed East with glutinous rice and spiced meats in a lotus leaf. They ordered the free-flow beer and white wine for 700 *baht.*

The view of the river also diverted them. Looking at the boats drifting by, Quinn talked about the tricks of river sailing. Kay reminisced about her early love for travel. A graduation trip to Paris, and seeing Notre Dame on the Seine, had started it all, she told Quinn.

As the sun slipped into the Chao Phraya, the sky turned magenta and then a soft amber. The running lights of the passing boats twinkled red and green, port and starboard, left and right, off the placid water. It looked hopeful to Quinn and helped him relax even more.

They couldn't help themselves. As soon as they got back to their room, Quinn flipped on the television for an update on what was happening in the streets. A breaking news report said the demonstrators had been dispersed by an overwhelming police and army response. Forty-some protestors had been injured seriously enough to require hospitalization, and hundreds more had been arrested.

At some point deep in the night, Quinn woke up on the couch and saw that Kay had turned off the TV and was asleep in one of the canopied beds. He slipped into the other one.

BY SIX THE NEXT morning, Quinn had turned on the news again, muting it until Kay finally stirred and joined him.

"What's happening?"

"No one was killed. But lots were injured. Some of them badly."

All the news flashes reported that order had been restored and most roads were open again. Videos of the Democracy Monument showed traffic flowing smoothly. The detritus of the blockade—discarded protest signs, spent tear-gas canisters—littered the sidewalks, and the generals were warning of a more lethal response should the demonstrators not stand down immediately.

They checked out of the hotel with others heading for the airport. Cabs seemed in short supply, and a liveried bellman went out onto busy Oriental Road to whistle one down. He seemed down to his last shrill tweet when one finally veered over and stopped.

The driver sped through mostly empty streets, screeching around corners and blaring his horn. More tanks and armored personnel were blocking intersections; troops raised their rifles when speeding cars got too close.

"It's like *The Year of Living Dangerously*," Quinn said as they zigzagged through traffic.

Glancing over at him, Kay said, "You make a pretty good Mel Gibson after all."

By the time they got back to Chiang Mai, there was apparently an uneasy truce in Bangkok, according to the television news reports Quinn now watched religiously, forgoing the American sports updates on his Fubo feed.

"Let me check on Tee," he said as soon as they returned to the office.

Tee picked up on the first ring. "Was just going to call you with an update, *Kuhn* Jack." In the background, Quinn could hear the sound of nails being pounded into wood.

"So how's it going?" Quinn meant it to be an open-ended question.

"Great. The local crew is really getting into it, and I'm meeting lots of young internationalists at the hotel."

"Are you keeping up with events in Bangkok?"

"The demonstrations? Of course. The military won, and it's quiet again. At least for now."

"Better to stay away."

"Sure. I'm fine here for now. As *Khun* Roy would say, 'Everything is copacetic.'"

CHAPTER TWENTY-THREE

Independence Day

Jane Harmon, the American consul, called Quinn at the office a few days later.

"We heard back from Amerasian Child Find, the *luk kreung* group in Colorado Springs. No match for Roy's DNA, I'm afraid. I'll bring the report to the Fourth of July celebration. You're going, right?"

"Of course."

"And Kay too?"

"I think so."

After much back and forth, Daryl had gotten his new posting. He had lobbied hard for Ukraine, but in the end, he'd been offered Azerbaijan.

"Daryl said Baku has a nice beach on the Caspian," Kay told Quinn and Phen.

There was no farewell dinner at the club. Just coffee and donuts at the consulate for staff. Daryl filed divorce papers in Arlington on the way to his new assignment.

The Independence Day celebration started at noon with the boom of a ceremonial cannon. The consulate was all decked out for a party. The courtyard was festooned with red-white-and-blue bunting hanging from every window, and small American flags lined the walkways. Smoke wafted from barbecues grilling hot dogs and hamburgers. Side tables offered relish, ketchup, and mustard along with soft rolls and American potato chips. Volunteers in a tent with a humming generator were dispensing chocolate and vanilla ice cream cones. Couples perambulated in time to the Sousa marches on the public-address system. Uncle Sam wobbled by on stilts.

Major Clive Purcell, in a Union Jack shirt and a straw boater, was shouting to any American who would listen, "Happy Independence Day. All is forgiven!" Tickets for free Budweiser, two per adult, had been provided at the door, and it appeared the Major had already used his. Maybe one of Mrs. Purcell's as well.

The festivities commenced with the presentation of colors by the VFW honor guard that had officiated at Balmer's funeral. Then came the singing of the national anthem, led by the skinny vet Quinn thought of as Beanpole but whose nametag said Earl Scruggs. He had a beautiful tenor voice. Those unfamiliar with the words read from the lyrics included in the program. Everyone tried.

Quinn figured Bill Smith, the VFW post commander, would have been part of the colors, but he was nowhere in sight. After waiting for Scruggs to finish accepting kudos on his fine voice, he asked him, "Where's Bill?"

"Old Bill's not doing so good," Scruggs sighed. "The docs at Chiang Mai Ram say he has some kind of bad cancer. Lymphoma, maybe? He's going back to the States for treatment. They've done all they can here. Some place in Texas, I think."

"That's going to be expensive. Do you think he was right? Was it Agent Orange that got him?"

"That's what he thinks. The consulate's helping him file a Veterans claim."

"Dick Collins isn't working on it, is he?"

"No. They got a new guy. Boohra type. Afghanistan vet. He seems interested."

"Good. I did an internet search on Agent Orange after

talking to you guys. I just found a Board of Veterans Appeals decision for a guy who humped Agent Orange onto planes at one of the bases in Thailand, like you guys did. After a bunch of denials, the board granted him a service connection for Non-Hodgkin's lymphoma. Now he's getting free care and a couple thousand dollars a month in compensation. I'll help on Bill's case. I have the citation."

"That's right, you're a lawyer."

Quinn paused only briefly. "Maybe so. What's the new guy's name?"

"I don't remember."

"I'll find him."

"You'd better hurry."

Scruggs gave Quinn a half-hearted salute and retreated into the crowd just as Jane Harmon approached.

"There you are," she said.

She reached into the bulky shoulder bag she always seemed to carry and pulled out a fat manila envelope.

"Roy's report," she said gently, handing it to Quinn. "Forensics was able to retrieve some DNA from the bone fragments, but they couldn't find any matches on the database. Seems no one is looking for him, Jack. Our guys got Roy's army records from the National Archives. They show he was discharged in San Diego, and we tried to track down his family. Nothing. Zilch. That's the end of the line for Roy, I'm afraid."

"Maybe not, though. Roy always told me that as long as someone remembers you, you're still alive. As alive as you and I are here, right now. Thomas Merton says that only in imagination does one become real. I believe that. And we'll remember Roy for a long time."

"I get it. But it's got to be a whole lot easier to live on if you leave a few descendants behind."

"His son is probably alive somewhere. DNA is powerful stuff. Maybe he thinks of his dad sometimes."

Quinn was suddenly overwhelmed by a sense of gratitude. He thought of his own two daughters, and their DNA, and his part in its alchemy. And his love for them and, despite trying not to make it about him, his pride.

A small group of American expats had gathered around Jane Harmon, crowding closer and closer as they waited for her to finish talking with Quinn. Most had questions. One complained about Medicare co-payment costs going up. Another expressed his opinion on the hoax of global warming. A third asked about the stability of the Thai government, a question she deftly deflected.

"We're here to celebrate," she said. And then, to Quinn, "Duty calls."

As she moved on, her constituents tagging along behind her, Kay joined him. After a few moments of companionable people watching, Quinn said, "Look, there's Derek."

"I figured he'd be here."

Derek had spotted them too and came over, limping a bit. Below his tattered cargo shorts, he wore a serious knee brace.

"Can't run as fast as I once could," he said when Quinn started to ask about it. Which raised all sorts of questions about where he had been and what he had been doing, none of which Quinn or Kay asked. "I think I'm going to hang it up," Derek went on. "Close the Press Club, retire for real. I'm thinking of moving back to Hong Kong, where there's some stability."

Quinn assumed Derek was joking, but you never could be sure.

Scanning the crowd again, Kay said, "Look, there's Tee!" as he entered the courtyard with his parents. Standing on her toes, she gave him a hearty wave.

Tee said something to his parents and rushed over.

"I should have called to tell you I was coming down from Tak. Last-minute decision."

"Never mind, we're just glad you're here," said Kay, giving Tee a hug.

"Doing great work up there," Quinn added. Tee had been sending regular reports with photos, just as Balmer had. The project was, as expected, progressing without a hitch.

"Ready for another project when this one's done?" Kay asked. There was hope in her voice.

"No, *Ah* Kay. I'm heading to Bangkok for the fall semester at Thammasat University, like I said."

Kay seemed disappointed but not surprised.

"Don't worry, Aunt Kay, the political situation is getting back to normal in Bangkok. The troubles are over, at least for a while."

"From what I'm reading, it sounds like the demonstrators won," Quinn said. "Pardons, elections, even a new constitution maybe...."

"Promises. All promises. We're in for the long haul."

"Like the Long March?"

"Not same same, *Kuhn* Jack," Tee said with a smile. He nodded toward a table at the edge of the crowd. "My parents are here," he said, pointing them out.

"And Phen," said Kay, who saw her sitting at the table. "She told me she was coming. I didn't know it was with you." She slapped Tee a high five.

"We've gotten to know each other better," Tee said. "What with all my work with GTEF and all."

"Always the last to know," said Quinn.

Tee's father smiled and motioned them over. Tee's mother held up the pin with the crossed Thai and American flags she'd received at the door.

"*Sabai dee, mai*? Are you well?" Quinn asked as they approached.

"*Sabai dee*," Tee's mother nodded, making room at the table.

Just then, Colonel Prasong Wongsarat strolled by. He seemed his usual ebullient self, to Kay and Quinn anyway. To them, he offered *wais* followed with solid handshakes. To Tee, he gave a fingers flip to his cap that was more a salute than a greeting. He didn't stay to chat.

"Gotta work the room," he said.

The celebration went on for hours, and Kay and Quinn stayed until the very end. The finale was a display of booming fireworks that looked like purple and pink chrysanthemums lighting up the night sky. The crowd responded with oohs and aahs.

As they watched the fireworks, Kay said, "I've been thinking, Jack. Maybe it's time for me to go home."

"What? Why?"

"Maybe I should try to settle down to a normal life. I could go back to Raleigh and see if I can teach at the college."

"That didn't work out so well last time, as I recall."

"No. You're right, it didn't."

"I can't believe you mean it, Kay. You know the foundation wouldn't survive without you." He paused. "And here I was planning to stay on."

"Really. For how long?"

"At least as long as you are."

"Jack Quinn, that sounds like a commitment."

"Could be," Quinn said, but he was pretty sure that it was.

EPILOGUE

AFTER SEVENTY YEARS ON the throne, King Bhumibol Adulyadej died in 2016. The country still grieves his loss. Student demonstrations continue, with calls for free and fair elections, reform of the monarchy, elimination of political corruption, and recognition of the country's LGBTQ community. The U.S. government has begun construction of a $300 million consulate on the river. Tee is a lawyer in Bangkok and is considering running for Parliament, representing Chiang Mai Province, as a member of the progressive Move Forward Party. Since COVID, Jack and Kay have been working from the house they rent in Seattle. They talk with Phen every day but can't wait to get back to the GTEF and Chiang Mai. Replacing Roy Balmer is still an ongoing struggle—with each project, they find lots of enthusiasm, too many soft hands. Teddy Dingle sends a Christmas card from England every year.

ACKNOWLEDGMENTS

THANKS TO MY WIFE, SHEILA, for her encouragement and patience during the long writing process. Thanks to Professor Toni Graham, at Oklahoma State University, who taught me how to write. Thanks to Pamela Feinsilber, editor extraordinaire. Thanks to book designer Jay Gilman, who put my words into book form, and illustrator Rich Sigberman, who created a cover that adds to my story. Thanks to English teachers everywhere. And tremendous thanks, always, to the people of Thailand who welcomed me.

ABOUT THE AUTHOR

HARRY DEERING GREW UP in Seattle, Washington. After graduating from Seattle University, he attended law school at King Hall, University of California at Davis. Then, in 1969, during the Vietnam War, he was drafted and stationed at a U.S. Army base in northeastern Thailand, thus beginning a long relationship with the country, its culture, and its people.

He spent his career working in San Francisco for the civil rights division of the U.S Department of Education as a senior program director. Over the years, he returned to Thailand again and again. When he retired, in 2007, he worked for a few years with a nonprofit organization in Chiang Mai that provided educational assistance to children in the hill tribes of the Golden Triangle, in northwestern Thailand where the borders of Thailand, Laos, and Myanmar, or Burma, meet at the confluence of the Mekong and Ruak rivers.

He and his wife, Sheila, live in Marin County, California. They love world travel and spending time with their four grandchildren. This is his first book. He is working on his second one.